# FORGIVEN

**Center Point
Large Print**

Also by Shelley Shepard Gray
and available from Center Point Large Print:

Sisters of the Heart Series
*Wanted*
*Hidden*

# FORGIVEN

## Sisters *of the* Heart
### BOOK THREE

## SHELLEY SHEPARD GRAY

CENTER POINT PUBLISHING
THORNDIKE, MAINE

This Center Point Large Print edition
is published in the year 2009 by arrangement with
Avon Books, an imprint of HarperCollins Publishers.

This book is a work of fiction. The characters,
incidents, and dialogue are drawn from the author's
imagination and are not to be construed as real.
Any resemblance to actual events or persons,
living or dead, is entirely coincidental.
The text of this Large Print edition is unabridged.
In other aspects, this book may vary
from the original edition.
Printed in the United States of America.
Set in 16-point Times New Roman type.

ISBN: 978-1-60285-633-2

Library of Congress Cataloging-in-Publication Data

Gray, Shelley Shepard.
  Forgiven / Shelley Shepard Gray.
    p. cm. -- (Sisters of the heart ; bk. 3)
  ISBN 978-1-60285-633-2 (library binding : alk. paper)
  1. Amish--Fiction. 2. Large type books. I. Title.

PS3607.R3966F67 2010
813'.6--dc22

2009029146

Judge not, and ye shall not be judged. Condemn not, and ye shall not be condemned. Forgive, and ye shall be forgiven.

Matthew 6:14

Friendship is a lighted candle
Which shines most brightly
When all else is dark.

A bit of wisdom from
*The Wooden Spoon Cookbook*

*To Arthur and Lesley,*
*for more reasons than I could ever list.*

# Chapter 1

*Crack.*

Jerking awake, Winnie opened her eyes. What was that? It was most unusual to hear anything in the middle of the night. Their farm was miles away from the city. By and large, the only noise to echo around their home was the impatient bleating of Nellie the goat or one of the horses.

Her eyes slowly focusing, she turned to look at the clock on her bedside table. Two A.M. Maybe she had imagined it.

Winnie lay back down. Well, perhaps the good Lord had summoned her awake for no reason at all. Slowly, she closed her eyes and tried to relax and remember her prayers.

But then it came again.

From the cozy comfort of her bed, Winnie turned toward the window, the cotton sheets tangling around her legs as she shifted. Beyond the window, a fierce wind blew, creating an unfamiliar howl in the darkness.

Ah, a storm was coming in. Well, the horses wouldn't care for that much.

Just as she closed her eyes, another snap rang out. A sharp pop followed seconds later. Sharp and loud, like the clap of a rifle. Winnie bolted upright.

Something was terribly wrong.

Outside, a low roar floated upward from the

ground, mixing with the high, panicked scream of a horse.

Winnie ran to the window and pulled back the thick plain curtain. Shooting flames and clouds of smoke greeted her.

Oh, sweet heaven! The barn was on fire!

She clasped a fist to her mouth as she watched Jonathan frantically run to the barn. Flames ate the opposite side.

She grabbed her thick robe, then flew down the stairs. She opened the front door just in time to see her brother throw a blanket over the top of Blacky's head and lead him out. "Jonathan!" she called out.

He didn't so much as look her way—the rage of the fire had swallowed her words.

Smoke choked the sweet spring air. A chalky black haze blurred everything around her . . . mixing with the cool gray fog of the early March night. Winnie stood motionless, stunned, feeling like she'd stepped into a dream.

Another crack screamed through the near dawn, drawing her attention to the pens next to the barn, where the goat and chickens slept. She'd just lifted the lever to free the squawking hens when the sky was suddenly alight with flames. The force of the explosion threw her to the ground. Sparks and ash fell through the air as she pulled herself to her feet to run toward cover.

Winnie couldn't seem to move. The soles of her

bare feet burned, were blistered and hot. Smoke ran thick. Her chest tightened. She coughed, the sound of it echoing in her ears as her vision blurred. Blazing pieces of hot, burning wood nicked her back and shoulders, bringing her down—just as if the devil himself was behind her. The pain was fierce. Crippling.

Terrifying.

She was barely aware of Jonathan yanking her by her shoulders and pulling her to safety.

Jonathan watched his friend Eli Miller arrive at the farm just as an ambulance skidded to a stop in front of their farmhouse. After Jonathan motioned him forward, Eli hurried over. "Jonathan, I'm glad to see you whole and unharmed. I came as soon as I could. The flames of your barn lit up the night sky."

Jonathan knew there were a great many things he should say to ease his friend's worries. But his heart seemed to have no room left in it for others. He was too stunned about the barn. And too worried about Winnie.

But if Eli was bothered by his quiet, he didn't act like it. Looking around, he frowned. "Where're Winnie and Katie and the girls?"

"Katie took the girls to her parents' inn for the night, so they're safe, thank Jesus. But Winnie . . ." Jonathan pointed to the inside of the ambulance. "She is in there."

"In the ambulance?" Eli's normally assured manner faltered. "Is she hurt bad?"

"*Jah.* She's in . . . She's in poor shape."

"That's terrible news."

"It is." Jonathan wasn't surprised by his friend's reaction. For as long as he could remember, he and his family had known the Millers. Eli's brother Samuel and his sisters had played with Winnie when they were small, and Jonathan had helped their family with spring planting more than a time or two. Winnie was like another sister to Eli, just as Jonathan felt like an older brother to Eli's youngest brother, Caleb.

Eli attempted to control his voice. "What's wrong?" Staring at the last of the flames, he murmured, "Is she badly burned?"

"I think I got her out before she was too injured, but I'm not certain." Jonathan tried to school his features, but it was difficult. "Some boards must have hit her . . . she fell . . . her feet are in a bad way, too. One might be broken. I . . . I had to carry her away from the area." Pain-filled eyes teared up before he wiped them impatiently with a hastily bandaged fist. "She's a fair sight."

Around them, the barn was still smoking and animals were howling their displeasure. Eli grasped his arm. "What can I do?"

"Well, now, I . . ." The question seemed to push away a portion of Jonathan's shock. After looking at the charred remains surrounding them, he reached out to touch the shiny red side of the ambulance. "Would you go with her to the hospital? Would you mind leaving your brother Caleb alone?"—Jonathan stepped toward the barn, toward the crowd of firemen talking to a man dressed in a coat and tie—"I canna leave. I have to speak with these men. And Katie and the girls will likely return soon. I'll need to be here for them."

"Of course you need to be here for your daughters. And your wife."

*"Danke."* Even though there was so much trouble, Jonathan felt a rush of warmth at the thought of his new wife. Barely two months had gone by since he and Katie had exchanged their vows in front of the whole community.

"I'll be happy to travel with Winnie. Caleb's almost seventeen. He'll be fine on his own. I'll contact Samuel, too."

Jonathan nodded. *"Danke.* It will set my mind at ease, knowing that she's not alone. If Samuel could help, I'd be mighty grateful. I heard he helped out Ingrid and Ben when they were at the hospital, tending to Ben's heart problems."

"He'll want to help. He and Winnie have always been good friends, plus he lives not two blocks from the hospital."

Pure relief washed over Jonathan. "I never thought I'd say this, but right now I'm glad Samuel's been living with the English. It will be nice to have someone there for Winnie."

"I think so, too." Though it had been hard to see him go, Eli had never faulted his brother. Surprisingly, no one in their family had been terribly shocked when he'd announced that he wasn't ready to join the church. Sam had always been a bright and inquisitive man. He'd ached for knowledge and the university like most Amish men ached for the land.

"Between Samuel and me, we'll make sure Winnie is taken care of. Don't worry. Winnie's like my sister. I won't let anything happen to her."

Clasping Eli's hand, Jonathan nodded. "I'm grateful."

As the flashing lights of the ambulance switched on again, one of the workers reached out to pull the door shut.

"Wait." Jonathan stopped him. "This man is coming with you."

The attendant nodded. "Hop in."

"I'll call the Brenneman's Bed and Breakfast with updates as soon as I know something," Eli said as he scrambled in. "That's the closest phone, right?"

"*Jah.*"

"Sam and I will watch over her," Eli called out as he obediently sat where the attendant motioned him to go. Jonathan hardly had time to nod before the doors slammed shut and the ambulance set into motion.

The crowd of people surrounding what was left of

the barn got bigger and bigger. Not twenty minutes after the ambulance left, Katie and his daughters, Mary and Hannah, arrived in their black buggy. "Oh, Jonathan," Katie cried, the moment she helped the girls down. "I'm so sorry I wasn't here."

"I'm not. I'm glad your mother needed an extra pair of hands at the inn. I would have been terribly worried about you and the girls."

"One of the men called the inn. I heard about Winnie!"

"Eli is with her in the ambulance." He started to brush back a stray lock of her hair but stopped when he caught sight of his sooty hands. "I was afraid to leave here."

"Eli will look after her."

Leaning down, he gave both Mary and Hannah fierce hugs.

"You smell like smoke!" Hannah cried.

"Everything does, but we'll be okay."

After another round of tearful hugs, Katie's mother, Irene, arrived. With easy efficiency, she led the girls into the house to prepare coffee and muffins for everyone. Jonathan knew before long, the yard would be filled with horses and buggies. Friends and neighbors would come from miles around to lend their support.

But no one helped ease his tension like his wife. "Katie, I hardly know what to do," he murmured after he'd told her about Winnie and her possible injuries.

"You don't need to know," she said without a pinch of doubt in her words. "The Lord will watch over Winnie, and He will take care of us, too." With a faint smile, she waved a hand around them. "He already has, wouldn't you say?"

Jonathan believed in the Lord with everything inside of himself. But that didn't stop his feeling completely lost. Gathering up his courage, he admitted, "I'm not sure what to do next."

"He'll let us know. You just have to believe and be patient."

After another hug, Katie left to go help her mother.

Jonathan watched her go, then looked at the crowd gathered. In spite of his fellow community members, he felt oddly alone. As the whole situation sunk in, Jonathan realized he had no words to describe his pain.

The fire marshal said he could wait inside if he wanted. But Jonathan didn't want that. He had to keep watching as the firemen battled the blaze.

After a bit, Katie's brother, Henry, stood by him, holding a mug. "Katie sent this out to you. A few sips might do you good."

Experimentally, Jonathan sipped. Henry was right. The steaming beverage did taste good. The hot liquid warmed his insides and the strong brew provided him with a much-needed jolt. *"Danke."*

As they stood together, staring at the smoldering ashes, Henry spoke again. "What happened?"

"I'm not altogether sure. I heard a loud pop. Once, years ago, my grandfather told me about the fire that struck their farmhouse. The noises I heard were ones he'd described. As fast as I was able, I got up and went to fetch Blacky."

"My *daed*'s over with the animals now, checking them out," Henry said. "Others are coming to help, I'm sure."

Jonathan expected nothing less. "I'll be grateful for the help." Thinking back to the fire, he said, "It spread something fierce. I could hardly believe it. A large explosion burst the side of the barn, whether it was from the hay or a container of kerosene, I don't know."

Henry was prevented from saying any more when the fire marshal returned, his expression grim. "Mr. Lundy, we'll do some more checking as soon as things have cooled down and the sky lightens up, but I'm afraid things don't look good."

"I don't imagine it would—my barn's gone," Jonathan said dryly.

"No, that's not what I mean." The tall thin man tugged at his necktie. "Mr. Lundy—"

"Jonathan, please."

"Jonathan, I hate to be the one to tell you this, but I'm afraid a cigarette caused this." After he said the words, he looked Henry's way, as if for help.

Jonathan didn't understand. Maybe the smoke was finally gettin' to him? "I don't smoke. No one here smokes cigarettes."

"All the same, it looks to be what happened."

Beside him, Henry cleared his throat. "Say again?"

If anything, the marshal looked even more uncomfortable. "What I'm trying to say . . . is that we found traces of a lighter and cigarettes near the back of the barn. We'll know more information in the morning, but it looks as if someone ran away in the back field as soon as the fire started. This fire might have been an accident, but it was definitely started from someone's carelessness, not by a force of nature."

"Cigarettes?" Henry repeated.

Behind them, Katie dropped the mug of coffee she'd been bringing out to her brother. Her gasp, along with the clang of broken pottery, brought Jonathan Lundy out of his trance.

His barn was gone. His sister was badly burned. Someone had been on his property without his knowledge.

Meeting the fire marshal's gaze, Jonathan looked him square in the eye. "You are right. This is a mighty bad happening. A mighty bad happening, to be sure."

# Chapter 2

Sam Miller rushed down the third-floor hallway of Adams Community Hospital, to the obvious irritation of the nurses on duty.

"Sir!" one called out. "Sir, this is a *hospital.*"

"I know." He raised a hand in apology, but kept on going. He'd finally spotted Eli.

His brother was sitting ramrod straight in the miniscule waiting area near a narrow window, a fuzzy television screen, and a waxy-looking potted plant. Sam exhaled. "Eli."

Eli jerked toward him, relief replacing the lines of weariness around his mouth when he saw his brother. "Sam."

His brother could ride rings around him on a horse, outwork him in the fields, and was one of the most upstanding, direct-talking men he knew. However, among the English, Eli was a babe in the woods.

Eli stood up and hugged Sam close for a moment, just like he used to do when they were small. "It's good to see ya. I'm glad you could come so quickly."

"I got here as fast as I could."

"You came. That's what counts."

As orderlies pushed carts and nurses and doctors strode by, their expressions filled with determination, Sam concentrated on his brother. "How are you doing? How's Winnie? Is Caleb here, too?"

"No. I let him stay home. As for me, I'm all right—it's Winnie that I'm wondering about. Samuel, I can't get any information. I tell you, finding out the truth here is near impossible." Directing a scowl down the hall, Eli added, "Every time I get up and ask a question, those nurses act like I'm bothering them."

Clasping Eli's arm, Sam took the seat next to him. "How long have you been here?"

"Hours. Since daybreak."

"Would you like me to speak to the nurses now? Or just wait with you?" The last thing Sam wanted to do was offend his older brother.

"Find out what you can, wouldja?"

"I'll be right back," he promised, already standing.

"I don't understand why they won't allow me to see Winnie."

"Maybe there's a good reason. I'll see what I can do."

Backtracking to the nurses' station he'd hurriedly passed just minutes before, Sam directed his attention to the most friendly-looking of the nurses. "Excuse me. My brother and I are concerned about a patient. Winnie Lundy?"

The nurse stepped close enough for him to read her name badge. Rebecca. "What do you need to know?"

"More than we know now, which is nothing."

Smiling slightly, he leaned forward a bit. "Rebecca, can you tell me how she's doing?"

"Not yet." Little by little, her frosty demeanor thawed. "We're waiting for the doctor's report."

"How long might that be? My brother's been here for hours."

"I'm sorry, sir—"

"He's worried. Certainly you understand that."

After pausing for a moment, she picked up the phone. "I'll do some checking and get back to you."

Sam hated the runaround. But worse, he hated his brother getting the runaround. "When might that be?" he pressed.

She looked put out. "Within the hour."

"I don't know if I did much better, Eli," Sam said when he made his way back to the set of orange vinyl chairs. "However, I did get one of the nurses to promise she'd fill us in as soon as she could. She promised we'd hear something within an hour."

Eli slumped. "That's something, I suppose. I hate the idea of poor Winnie sitting somewhere by herself."

"She might not be. She's probably getting seen by a number of doctors and nurses and that's why we can't disturb them."

"Perhaps."

Hoping to take Eli's mind off the terrible wait, Sam said, "Tell me again what happened. Jonathan's barn caught fire?"

"*Jah.* It was a terrible thing. Flames shot up something fierce, and then all the hay in the loft ignited. I overheard some of the English say it looked like a bomb. All the commotion woke me up."

"Is the whole barn gone?"

"Oh, *jah.* Well, enough that it can't be saved." Eli shook his head sadly. "A lifetime of work, gone in an instant."

"That's terrible."

"It is. A shame."

Sam reckoned his brother was right. It was a shame. While it had been a good three years since he'd been to the Lundys', he knew the farm well. Lush, green, and well kept, it was a showcase for the area. The barn, with its green metal roof, was especially eye-catching.

For a fire to have burnt the whole thing down, it was almost as if part of history had been wiped away. He remembered their father talking about the barn raising as if it had been yesterday.

Eli leaned back in his chair. "It was a fair sight, to be sure. The flames lit up the sky. When I arrived, Jonathan had already gotten the animals out, but Winnie was in the ambulance. She's been burned, and I think maybe her foot is broken. I don't know what else." He turned to him. "You remember Winnie, don't you? Black hair, dimples in her cheeks?"

Sam recalled a skinny girl with too much on her

mind. But it had been years since he'd seen her. "Of course. She was a few years behind me at school."

"I had forgotten that. Don't know why." Circling back to the original problem, Eli muttered, "I wish someone would come out and tell us what is going on. I'm not used to sittin' around."

"I know you're not."

Sam, however, was far more used to waiting on other people. Government lines, post office lines, shoot, even the lines at the grocery store. He was used to either texting people on his cell phone or making do. Eli, so used to the insular life in their community, was not.

Eli worried his black felt hat. "I promised Jonathan I'd look out for her, and I know he's waiting for some answers. I feel bad I haven't called him." Frustration tinged his words as he gave up trying to make sense of it all.

"Waiting seems to be the norm for everything nowadays."

"Maybe so. I'm fortunate to have a brother who will still drop everything to help him at a moment's notice."

The praise embarrassed Sam. Instinctively, he half waited for Eli to point out the obvious. Yes, he'd come today to help. But what about all the other times Eli had needed him but he hadn't been around?

Sometimes he felt like he'd abandoned his

family, leaving the order. It was hard to come to terms that he'd picked an education over living closer to his family and joining the church. Though no one had ever *said* they resented him for leaving, Sam wondered if they did.

After another twenty interminable minutes, the nurse he'd spoken with approached them. Sam jumped to his feet. "Rebecca, have you found out any information yet?"

"Only a little bit. I've been waiting for Dr. Sullivan to give us the okay to accept visitors. After he saw Winnie in emergency, he went on rounds. However, I just got a hold of him and he gave the okay for a brief visit."

"Thank you, that's very good news."

"How is Winnie?" Eli asked.

Rebecca flipped through the papers clipped to the top medical chart she was holding. "She's just been moved to a private room. It looks like she's sustained a number of cuts and abrasions, and some burns to her legs. Her right foot is also fractured."

"Poor Winnie," Eli muttered.

"If you'll follow me, I'll take you both to her room."

Taking a calming breath, Eli nodded. "That would be fine."

Luckily, they didn't have far to go, just a few feet down one gray-checkered hallway, then another couple of yards down a second, this one with blue and green squares. Around them, stainless steel racks and bins lined the walls. The sharp, pungent smell of lemon-scented bleach filled the air.

Finally they arrived. "Here is her room. Number five-forty-one."

Eli already had his hand on the door handle. "Thank you."

"You're welcome. Remember, don't stay long, and don't be too worried if she's groggy. They've given her some medicine for her pain."

Pointing to a brown plastic chair outside her room, Sam said, "I'll wait out here, Eli."

"There's no need. Winnie would be pleased to see you, I think."

In her condition? Sam doubted that. Lately, he hadn't met a woman who appreciated seeing someone new without looking her best. "I don't—"

"Come, now. I don't want to stand here holding the door forever."

Reluctantly, Sam followed his brother in, hoping to stay in the back shadows and then slip out when the two of them got to talking.

But he had a hard time concealing his surprise when he did see Winnie Lundy. She certainly looked very different than he remembered her. Even lying down, she looked tall and lean. Eyes the color of a fading winter day set off ivory skin.

Those eyes widened when she focused on them. "Eli?"

"Yes. I'm here. Sam, too."

Embarrassed, Sam held up a hand.

"Don't stay too long," the nurse murmured once more after checking Winnie's vital signs and slipping out the back door. Sam edged closer. Ready to leave the moment it seemed suitable.

With his usual way, Eli moved to her bedside quickly. "So, how are you feeling?"

"Not so good." She frowned. "My foot hurts."

"Only one?" Eli teased.

"Both." With a frown, she glared at her feet. One was covered in protective gauze and bandages, the other in a temporary cast.

Eli raised his brows and whistled low. "Your feet and legs got the worst of it, I'm afraid. What did the doctor tell you?"

Winnie frowned. "That I'm going to be here for a few days. He said burns are prone to infection, and since I'm going to have a difficult time walking I need to let my body heal a bit here."

*"Das gut."*

"No, it's not." Obviously agitated, Winnie gripped a handful of white sheet, almost as if she'd like to be choking it. "The last thing everyone needs is for me to be in the hospital. Jonathan and Katie are going to be busy enough."

"I came for Jonathan. Samuel is going to help, too. That's why we have friends and family, *jah*?"

"Yes, but I know you shouldn't be spending your days here either. You've got plenty to do, too, Eli. I know it's planting season."

"*Jah,* those seedlings will wait for no man. I'm gonna go back tomorrow, but I'm sure Katie will visit tomorrow for a bit. And Sam here has promised to keep an eye on you for us all. He's going to visit with the doctors, too. Sam—" He looked around. "Sam?"

"I'm here."

"You look like you were about to leave. Come closer, Winnie can hardly see ya."

Feeling once again like the little brother tagging along, Sam approached. "Hi, Winnie. I'm sorry about the barn and your injuries." To his surprise, she smiled, showcasing the pair of dimples Eli had mentioned.

"Samuel Miller, you are a sight for sore eyes."

Eli chuckled. "I'm sure he'd rather you saw him with good eyes."

Sam couldn't help it. He met Winnie's gaze and smiled, just like they used to do years ago, before they'd grown up and changed. "It's been a long time since we've seen each other. You weren't around when I came to visit my family in the fall."

"I was in Indiana."

"Well, I'm glad to see you. I wish we were visiting under other circumstances."

"I do, too." After a pause, Winnie looked beyond him to his brother. "So, how is Jonathan? Is he hurt, too?"

"I don't think so."

"What about the barn? The animals?"

27

"I haven't called to get any information. I've been waiting to hear news about you."

"Will you go call?"

"Winnie Lundy, you are as bossy as ever."

"I'm only worried about the farm and my family."

"You should be thinking about healing, don'tcha think?"

"I can't get better until I know how everyone else is. Go call, would you?"

"I will, when I find a phone—"

"You can use my cell phone," Sam interrupted, eager to be back in the conversation. Pulling it out of his jeans pocket, he carefully showed his brother how to dial the number and press send. "You'll have to use it outside, though. Hospitals don't take kindly to people using cell phones in the halls."

Looking determined, Eli nodded. "I'll go call right now. If you're sure you don't mind being left again."

"I'll be all right."

With a start, Sam realized that Winnie thought he was going to leave the room, too. Had she really thought so little of him? "I'll stay with you. That is, if you don't mind."

Pulling the sheets a little more securely around herself, Winnie shook her head. "I don't mind."

Sam sat in the chair next to the hospital bed. "Is there anything I can do for you?"

A dimple appeared. "You mean besides gettin' me outta here? No."

"Did you understand everything the doctors said?" he asked gently. He could only imagine how scared she must be. The sterile hospital was a far cry from her usual environment. "I can speak to them for you."

"I can talk to doctors, Samuel."

"I didn't mean—"

Immediately, regret filled her eyes. "Listen. I am grateful for your help. I imagine Eli is, too."

"I'm happy to help."

"But, surely, you have other things you'd rather be doin'?"

Sam swallowed hard. It was obvious that Winnie felt he'd moved on and now no longer cared very much for the people he grew up with. It was evident in her voice, in the way she looked at him.

Sam had essays to read and five students to mentor at the college, not to mention the usual work on his research programs. But all that paled compared to the look of need in this woman's eyes.

Eli walked back in. "I spoke with Katie's mother, Irene. She said all the animals are safe, and Jonathan is no worse for wear. Only the barn is a complete loss."

Winnie pursed her lips. "We'll have to tear it down and begin again."

"That we will," Eli said. "Irene said Jonathan was pretty upset about it, not so much because of the work required but because your father had built the barn."

*"Jah,"* Winnie said with tears in her eyes.

"Jonathan's mighty worried about you. I told Irene I'd call back when I spoke with the doctor, but that Winnie was awake."

"I'm right here, you know. I could tell you how I'm feeling."

Sam looked at Winnie and grinned. "You never were meek, Winnie. Even when we used to play games at school, you always insisted on being in the thick of things. I guess some things never change."

With a quick glance at Sam, Winnie blushed. "Some things do." After clearing her throat, she said, "Eli, come sit down and talk to me. The last thing I remember is the barn exploding."

"That would be the hay catching on fire."

Sam nodded in response. As Eli talked about the excitement of riding in an ambulance, Sam noticed Winnie's eyes drift shut. The ordeal was taking its toll on her, and most likely, the painkillers were making her sleepy as well.

When Eli continued to prattle, Sam touched his arm. "It's time to go."

"You think so? We've only been in here a few moments."

"Look," Sam pointed out. Winnie's eyes had drifted shut.

Eli's cheeks flushed. "All my talking wore her out, I'm afraid."

Giving in to impulse, Sam nudged his older brother. "Yep, you always were a bore, Eli."

As he hoped, humor lit his brother's expression again. "Not all of us have a fancy education, you know." Once out in the hall again, Eli leaned his head back against the cool tiles on the wall. "It's been a terribly long day."

"How about I take you back to my place and you can get some sleep? I'll come back just in case Winnie wakes up."

"You don't mind?"

"Not at all."

"Then I'll take you up on it." He looked around. "Where do you think the doctor is? I want to know what is going on with Winnie."

"I'll check in with him when I get back. Most likely, he's doing rounds or something."

"I suppose." They took the stairs down to the parking area. Moments later, they were in Sam's Ford truck.

Eli might have been Amish, but he had a typical man's interest in all things mechanical. They spent the drive to Sam's place discussing the engine, gas mileage, and other details about his vehicle. Only when they parked in front of Sam's condo did he realize they'd spoken in Pennsylvania Dutch the whole time.

Funny how that came back to him without even realizing it.

"My place isn't much," he warned as he

unlocked the door. "It's just two bedrooms, a kitchen, and a place to sit."

Eli looked around with interest. Stepping forward, he pressed a hand against Sam's ancient corduroy couch. "Good enough for me."

"Want something to eat? I have some turkey."

"Turkey's good. Thanks."

Together, they made sandwiches, then ate them with pickles and tall glasses of tea. Now that their immediate concerns about Winnie were abated, Eli took time to fill Sam in on the latest news about their parents and sisters, Beth, Kristen, and Toria. Just the week before, their parents had taken a bus to Lancaster to check on their grandparents. Mamm's parents' health was failing, and though the timing wasn't the best, with planting season just around the corner, the trip had to be taken.

Sam was thankful for all the latest news. He did write to his parents once a week, and tried to visit with the family at least once a month, but that was not always possible, given everyone's schedules. Right as they finished their sandwiches, Sam realized that Eli hadn't filled him in on their brother Caleb. "Is Caleb all right?"

For the first time, Eli frowned. "I don't know. He's been restless and secretive."

"He's seventeen. All boys are like that, especially during their *rumspringa*. I sure was."

"Maybe." Leaning back, Eli said, "I remember you feeling torn. All of us knew it was because you loved schooling so much. Even the bishop knew you had a great mind and were anxious to learn." He shook his head, considering. "But I don't get the same feeling about Caleb, and neither does Mamm or Daed."

"What do you think is going on?"

"Foolishness."

"What kind? Has he been drinking beer? Staying out too late?"

"If it was just that kind of thing, I don't think anyone would notice much. No, his behavior seems different. He's pushing our boundaries."

"What does Daed say?"

Eli raised an eyebrow. "What do you think? Nothing. Our father never shares his worries." Crumpling up his napkin, he added, "And, well, Caleb is their late-in-life child. Sometimes I think they turn a blind eye toward his activities. Far more than when you and I were teenagers."

"Sometimes I wish he'd tell us more. I never know what he's thinking."

"Maybe one day he'll share more. Not yet, though." Stifling a yawn, Eli stood up and stretched. "I best get some sleep. I won't be much use to Winnie if I can't keep my eyes open."

"Don't worry. I'm leaving now to sit with her. And I'll continue to sit with her tomorrow, too, after you go on home."

"You don't mind?"

"It's the least I can do. Use my phone and call

33

my cell when you wake up. I'll give you an update."

"I should probably call the Brennemans, too, and check in again."

"Call all the people you want, Eli. My phone is yours."

"Just plan on me having your bed for the night, brother. That's enough, I think."

After another wave goodbye, Sam walked to his truck, wondering why he felt such a need to help. Because of his older, steady brother who had always been there for him? Because Eli always supported him, even when Sam's wants and needs were so foreign to Eli's?

Or was he doing all this for Winnie, who he'd hardly known but had felt instantly drawn to?

After all this time.

# Chapter 3

"This place smells like the inside of a *shanshtah*," Katie murmured as they stood in front of what was left of the barn three days after it had gone up in flames.

"I wish it was only the chimney smell that concerned me," Jonathan replied. "Unfortunately, the odor is the least of our worries."

Yes, the air around them most certainly held the scent of ashes, but the pungent odor was nothing compared to the destruction of his barn. Though it hadn't burned completely down, more than half was gone. What remained looked so flimsy that it wasn't worth the risk of keeping. The whole structure was going to need to be torn down, then rebuilt. "I don't know how I'm going to set things to rights," he added.

"Luckily, you don't have to do anything on your own. Both our families are eager to help, as is the rest of the community, English and Amish. We're all praying, too, you know."

"I keep forgetting to count my blessings." Thinking of Samuel Miller's latest phone call, he said, "It is surely a blessing that Winnie is going to be better soon."

"When Anna and I visited her yesterday, she seemed almost like herself."

As he looked around at the extensive damage,

Jonathan couldn't help but shake his head in wonder. "It's a blessing that all our animals came through this, too. We didn't even lose a chicken."

"The Lord surely was looking out for us." Katie laid a hand on his shoulder. "He'll help us now, too, I think. And don't forget, we've got each other."

"I never forget that," he murmured as he shifted and turned to pull his wife into his arms. "Your love is my greatest blessing."

Yes, her love truly did warm his heart. On some mornings, when he woke to hear Katie already fussing in the kitchen, humming a tune, he could hardly believe they were now married.

What a whirlwind their courtship had been, too! Less than a year ago he was a lonely widower, who'd gone to Katie's home and asked if her parents could spare her for a time so she could help with Mary and Hannah while Winnie traveled to Indiana.

At first, things had been difficult—neither he nor the girls had been especially welcoming to her at first. But as days turned to weeks, a love between them all had bloomed. Next thing he knew, they were planning a wedding. Now they were a family. Obviously, the Lord knew he needed someone special in his life.

Together they entered the house, which was miraculously undamaged by either the fire from the barn or the water from the fire trucks. As soon as they entered the kitchen, Katie began to bustle about.

He took a seat at the worn table and took a moment to watch her. As usual, she fussed like a busy bee, wiping down already clean counters, filling a teapot with water, then placing it on the gas-powered range to boil, and neatly folding two towels that the girls must have used earlier in the day. Finally, she laid a particularly pleasing cake in front of him. "I made a sour cream cake early this morning. I thought you might enjoy a slice while we make plans."

"And how did you know plans were going to need to be made?" He'd purposely been vague about his worries, knowing she would try to shoulder all of the burdens.

She smiled as she picked up the knife and cut two generous pieces and placed them carefully on plates. "I heard the fire inspectors saying they'd be back today to visit with you. I guess we're going to have a lot to think about."

Biting into the warm, moist cake, he paused for a moment, just enjoying the simple goodness of the treat. After he put his fork down, he said, "I'm worried, Katie. I'm worried about Winnie and the animals and rebuilding and finding the time to rebuild. But I'm also terribly worried about the cause of the fire. The inspector said the culprit was most likely a tossed cigarette. It just doesna make sense. Who would be smoking in my barn?"

A dark shadow flickered across her face as she pushed her plate to one side. "Well, now. That is a difficult question. I'm not sure."

Something in her voice led Jonathan to believe that there was something she wasn't saying. "But you must have an idea, right?"

"Well . . . I might."

"Come now, Katie. Tell me what *you* think. Do you reckon it was maybe an English teen trying to find a place to get away?"

"All I know is that it wasn't me or you or Mary and Hannah."

Hastily swallowing his latest bite of cake, he looked at her frankly. Yes, his *frau* most certainly had an idea about the smoker in his barn. "Who do you think, Katie? I'm out of ideas. I've racked my brain, but for the life of me, I canna think of anyone who would even think of such a thing."

Reluctantly, she looked at him. "Maybe it was an Amish teenager," she said quietly. "Maybe someone was having a little smoke and something went terribly wrong. An accident. I don't think it was an *Englischer* teen. There are many other places to smoke and carry on besides an Amish farm. No . . . I reckon it was an Amish teen. An Amish boy or girl experimenting with smoking."

"That could never happen." No member of the community would lurk around other people's property. Besides, if it was someone who was

Amish, he would have come forward and admitted his mistake.

"Sure it could. We Amish aren't perfect, you know. We all make mistakes time and again."

He pushed away his plate. It no longer looked appetizing. "Yes, but . . ."

With a hard glare, she stopped his words. "Oh, honestly, Jonathan. Don't be so naïve. I smoked. I experimented."

She was such a perfect wife he sometimes forgot her dark history. "Well, you're the exception, Katie. I'm sure most Amish *kinner* don't act out like you did."

"Like me?"

"Jah, like you," he fired back. "Your running-around years were difficult—you've said so yourself. Neither Winnie nor I ever did the things you've admitted to doing."

"I thought you said you understood about my past," she said quietly. "I thought you forgave me."

"I have." Feeling frustrated, Jonathan reached for her hand. "I'm not angry with you, I'm just sayin' I don't think an Amish teen burned down my barn."

In a huff, she stood up. "Well, I think differently, not that you seem to want to listen to my views. Now, excuse me while I go tend to the girls' rooms." Like a whirling dervish, Katie jumped to her feet, slapped the cake plate onto a counter with a thump, then swirled toward the front hallway.

He called out to her before she disappeared completely. "Katie, what did I say?"

Her feet slowed. "It's not worth talking about."

"I think it is. I thought you were tryin' to teach me how to be more open. To communicate better!"

When she turned around, Jonathan noticed tears had filled her eyes. "Katie, please talk to me."

"Perhaps you could begin to listen with your ears and your heart. Don't say one thing and mean another."

"I wasn't doing that."

"I think you were. I think you said you forgave me, but you didn't really mean it."

Her words caught him off guard. Had he done that?

Before he could say a word, she spoke again. "Jonathan, perhaps you should do some thinking about whoever did this. The Bible asks us to forgive our sins, even those who sin against us. Are you going to be able to do that? Are you ever going to be able to really forgive whoever burned your barn, put your animals in danger, and sent your sister to the hospital?"

He was prevented from pursuing the discussion by a brief hard rap at the door. "That's the inspector," he said.

A flash of tenderness filled her gaze before she turned away. "You'd best go get the door, then."

After another hard rap, he opened the door to

the fire inspector. "Good afternoon, Mr. Grisson."

"Mr. Lundy, hello. Want to come out to the barn? I'd like your opinion on some things."

"I'll be right there," he said quietly, just before he donned his black hat and followed the fire marshal outside. Katie had given him a lot to think about. And, most importantly, he had a feeling she was right. He wasn't sure if he was ever going to be ready to forgive the person who trespassed and damaged his property.

That was a terribly hard realization to come to terms with.

Sam's cell phone chimed late Sunday afternoon, just as he was about to drive over to the hospital and check on Winnie again.

As soon as he answered, Eli spoke in a rush. "Samuel, I'm calling from the Brennemans'. I am worried about Caleb. Once again he is not here when he's supposed to be."

"Maybe he simply forgot the time. You remember how it was when we were teens," Sam said reasonably.

"No, it's more than that. I told him he needed to tend to his chores, no matter what else he did today. When I went out to the barn, the horses' stalls still hadn't been cleaned."

Now, that was worrisome. Their father had ingrained in all of them the importance of tending to responsibilities. He couldn't imagine Caleb had been taught any different. "Eli, do you think he's gotten into some kind of trouble?"

"I'm not altogether sure." Sounding weary, Eli added, "I was never interested in pushing boundaries like he is. Come to think of it, I was never too concerned with the outside world. And you, you just wanted to go to school."

That was a fair assumption. Learning had been his rebellion, and it had taken up a lot of his extra time. It had been a difficult and tough decision to discuss his desire to focus on learning instead of Amish life. "Learning how things worked was all I thought about. But Caleb isn't like us, is he?"

"He's more secretive—and used to more freedoms. Remember how we always had the girls to look after?"

"I never thought I'd ever be able to go anywhere without Beth," Sam said.

"I feel responsible, too, since Mamm and Daed are visiting our grandparents."

"When Daed comes back, you can speak to him." With a jolt, Sam realized that, indeed, that was how it was going to be. He'd had little to no part in raising Caleb—the boy had been still a child when he'd left home. Though they were brothers, sometimes he felt as if he was little more than a distant relation.

"One night last week . . . he came home drunk."

"All boys do that at least once, I imagine." He'd taught at the college long enough to know a bit of experimental drinking was the norm instead of the exception.

"I wonder . . ."

Sam clutched the phone tighter. "What?"

"It's nothin', just that . . ."

"What, Eli?" Sam was really starting to feel alarmed.

"Lord forgive me for even thinking this, but I don't trust Caleb right now. I'm afraid . . ." He closed his eyes. "I'm afraid he was involved with the fire."

Sam felt as if someone had punched him in the stomach. "You think?"

"I appreciate you not pushing off my fears. Samuel, ever since the fire, Caleb has seemed more withdrawn. He's not offered to go with me to help clean up. In fact, every time I mention the fire, he looks like he wants to escape." He cleared his throat. "Samuel, what are we going to do if it *was* Caleb who started the fire?"

"I don't know." That would be a terrible situation. He didn't know what he would do—or what he would say if Caleb found out that he and Eli suspected him of that.

Both situations would be hard to excuse.


"I won't have a boy of mine lazing around from sunup to sundown," his father called out from the buggy whose wheel he was repairing. "Get to work and stop your lollygagging."

David Hostetler hurried out to the barn, grabbed hold of his work gloves, and went where his *daed* had told him to go, to the back pasture. Weeds were threatening to choke the path to the pond creek. It was a sorry, awful job, pulling out weeds, cutting debris, then carting it away. As he tromped out, taking care to not step in the mud, he passed his two older brothers who were almost mirror images of their father.

"What were you doing over there, just sitting around in the sun?" Kenny asked. "Daydreaming?"

"No. I just lost track of time."

"You'd best start remembering or be prepared to be reminded," Anthony said.

Though Anthony was right, David didn't comment on it. Instead, he tucked his head down and kept walking. There was nothing to say, and nothing anyone expected him to say. He was the middle child in a family of eight. He never seemed to stand out. At least, not in any good way.

He picked up his pace. Finally, away from the prying eyes of his family, right next to the cool, trickling waters of Wishing Well Lake, he pulled off his glove.

The burns were painful, the skin raw and blistered. Days in hot stiff leather gloves only served to make things worse. The only good thing about his current chores in the fields were that if he worked his hands raw, no one would question where he got the burns, they'd only tease him for having soft hands, not work-hardened and tough.

But David would welcome that teasing, because it would mean that no one knew what he'd done. After slipping on his gloves, he grabbed hold of the scythe and swung the blade against the tall grasses.

The sting was almost welcome. Anything was better than thinking about the fire.

# Chapter 4

"We won't have to delay our wedding, do you think?" Anna Metzger asked as soon as Henry joined her on the front porch of the Brenneman Bed and Breakfast. Gazing toward the horizon, where just a few miles away the Lundy farm was situated, she murmured, "Is it appropriate to say our vows with everyone still recovering from the fire?" Recalling the heartbroken expressions on Jonathan and Katie's faces, she added, "Maybe we shouldn't celebrate such happy things right now."

Henry looked at her with concern. "You sound as if more is bothering you than the troubles at the Lundy farm. Is there a reason you're asking? Do you want to delay things?"

"Not at all. We've already waited so long."

"That we have."

When Henry held out his hand, Anna took it with pleasure. The moment his fingers curved around hers, she recalled the first time they'd held hands. A spark of awareness had run through her body, making her realize happiness might actually be possible. It had been an astonishing moment . . . for a time, she'd been sure happiness would never find her again.

Now, with his touch, warmth and comfort was in her life. Looking into his eyes, she shook her head. "I guess I just want everyone to be happy."

"I want that, too."

As they stepped down the four steps that led to the front porch, and walked along the neatly trimmed walkway to the surrounding gardens, Anna smiled. "I can't help but be envious of Katie and Jonathan. As soon as they knew they wanted to get married, they went and said vows. It all happened within months."

"They had different circumstances. After all, Katie already was Amish."

"Well, I'm Amish now, too," Anna said proudly. "And I think it is time I got married and was your wife." After entering the garden, she stepped away from her fiancé and wandered down the rows of budding plants. This garden was a tremendous source of pride for her—until she'd come to live at the inn, she'd never tried to grow even a single tomato. Now Henry's mother, Irene, entrusted her with much of the upkeep of the large garden.

When she stopped at a row of fresh herbs, fragrant aromas filtered around them, the smell of thyme, rosemary, mint, and parsley lighting her senses. Unable to stop herself, she knelt down and pulled two pesky weeds. "I feel like I've been waiting forever."

Maneuvering among the rows far more slowly, Henry sniffed a batch of dusky purple lavender, plucked a stray dandelion, then tossed it into her pile. When Anna looked at him approvingly, Henry chuckled. "It's just been a little over a year, Anna."

With a grimace, she attacked two thistles that had the misfortune of daring to bloom in the midst of three heirloom tomato plants. "Just what I said. Forever."

"Hardly that."

"It feels like forever when you're in love."

Pulling her hands back into the comfort of his own, he brushed his lips against her brow. "Oh, Anna. I love you, too. Now, don't worry. I'll make sure we won't delay the wedding. Katie and Jonathan will understand."

She loved it when he told her he loved her—she knew she'd never get tired of hearing sweet things from him, of hearing how much he cared about her. "I hope Winnie will understand, too. When Katie and I visited her, she looked to be healing, but still in some pain."

"Jonathan saw her yesterday. He said she was sitting up in bed."

"That's good. She must be feeling better."

"*Jah*—and listen to this—Samuel Miller called with news again last night. Winnie's physicians reported last night that they will be discharging her soon. Maybe even in a day or two." With a direct look, he said, "Then, of course, we'll need to help her get around with that cast. I have a feeling she's not going to want a few injuries to slow her down."

Just imagining Winnie attempt to do her usual routine with a cast on her foot made Anna smile. "You're right about that. She'll be warring with her injuries, for sure." As Anna thought of Henry's report, she mused, "So, Sam Miller was there again?"

"Yes."

"It sure is nice he's helping her so much at the hospital."

"It is."

Anna wished she knew more about what was going on between Winnie and Sam. When she and Katie had quizzed Winnie about him, her normally talkative friend had turned conspicuously closed-mouthed. "Have Sam and Winnie known each other a long time?"

"Yes, all of us have known each other all our lives. Samuel and I are the same age, with Winnie just a few years behind. Eli Miller is twenty-eight. Katie is a bit younger than you, just twenty."

"What a time you all must have had."

Henry treated Anna to a rare smile. "We sure did. We were constantly running through chores to play kickball or some such." He paused. "Lately, though, few of us have seen Samuel. He moved on, you know. Though we have lots in common, Samuel chose a different path." A dab of worry appeared between his brows. "I always thought he was happy to be living among the English. I hope Winnie isn't finding his views too strange."

"Well, it's certainly nice he's been so attentive. I know it's eased both Katie and Jonathan's minds to have him nearby."

"Like I said, he's known Winnie for many years."

"But they haven't seen each other much since Sam left the order. Why is he being so attentive? It seems out of place for him to be so concerned with Winnie's health."

"I don't think so. Katie's worrying about Mary and Hannah, Jonathan's got his work at the lumberyard and the cleanup at his place, and Eli's got Caleb and spring plowing," Henry pointed out practically. "Samuel, on the other hand, is right there. Even if he's not Amish, I'm sure he feels just as strongly as he ever did about being near family."

"Well, I'm probably reading too much into things. But I couldn't ignore how Winnie reacted when we brought up how much Sam was visiting. What if something wonderful was happening? What if they're falling in love? Winnie's had such heartache, not being able to find her right partner . . ."

Henry stopped tugging on a dandelion and frowned. "*Lieb?* Between Samuel and Winnie?"

"Don't act so surprised!"

Henry looked at her sharply. "I think smelling all this peppermint has gotten to you. They wouldn't be in love. They couldn't. Samuel's no longer a part of our world and . . ."

"Sure, they could," she interrupted. "Stranger things have happened. Look at you and me."

"I don't fancy being thought of as strange."

Anna looked at him sharply, then grinned as she caught his joke. Feeling better, she continued with her dreams. "I don't know, Henry. Just think, there's poor Winnie, stuck in the hospital with nothing to do. And Sam visits her all the time. Seems like the perfect time to grow a friendship."

"It's the perfect time to wish there was somethin' else to do besides sit in a drab hospital room, mark my words about that."

"Maybe . . . but maybe not."

"Ach. You have your head in the clouds, Anna Metzger. You need to be thinking about your wedding and our life together. Not Winnie and Samuel."

"But what if—"

"Nope. It won't."

As he leaned close to kiss her, Anna smiled. Well, Henry could deny it all he wanted, but Anna knew there was more on Winnie's mind than just injuries.

"Anna?" Henry whispered as his lips brushed her jaw.

"Mmm-hum?"

"Stop thinking and kiss me back."

That, at least, was something she was very sure she could do.


Now that the pain from the burns was subsiding, Winnie felt more at ease. Not only had it been hard to focus on anything other than finding relief, but the enforced time lying on her back had made the hours go by so slowly. She'd also hated being connected to so many tubes. It was embarrassing to have to ask the nurses for help to do most anything.

It had been difficult, feeling so terribly vulnerable.

Now that she wasn't on so many pain medications and her head was clear, Winnie's mood had brightened considerably. She could visit with whoever stopped by in her usual manner.

That was a good thing. She liked feeling in control and being aware of her surroundings, especially in an unfamiliar situation like the one she was in now.

Hospitals most certainly were not the place for her, though everyone had been as attentive as possible. The constant noise outside her door was jarring, as was the pungent smell of disinfectant. In addition, someone came to see her at least once an hour, to check her vital signs or to give her medicine.

At least the people who worked there were nice. The doctor, Dr. Sullivan, was mighty kind, too. He seemed to understand how scared she was, and he not only checked her injuries but stayed an extra moment or two and talked about things.

Now Winnie knew all about Dr. Sullivan's two grandchildren and his love for hiking. They'd begun to talk hiking trails around the area. Winnie had even promised to write him a list of her favorite spots up near Lake Erie. All of this had been much to his assistant's annoyance, Winnie was afraid. The younger Dr. Merchek was a man who kept a strict schedule and doled out smiles like expensive rewards.

Though the other patients she'd talked with complained bitterly about a constant stream of visitors, Winnie had become appreciative of it. Otherwise, she knew she would have caught herself worrying about Jonathan, Katie, and the girls, or wishing she could do something—anything—to try and help them out.

But of course, her only job was to try and get better and listen to what the doctors said.

Restlessly, she pressed the button on the television remote and watched the screen. A pair of women seated on a bright blue couch were talking about their children. One was terribly upset—it looked like no one could comfort her.

When a man in the audience yelled at them, Winnie pushed the channel changer. Oh, but she would never understand why so many people discussed their problems with strangers!

She'd just found a game show when a knock came at the door.

She looked up expectantly. Even a shot would be a welcome distraction from her boredom.

"Are you up for company right now?" came a muffled voice from behind the door.

Her heart got all fluttery. In quick order, she shut off the TV. "Sam?"

Cracking the door open, he poked his head in, his lovely light brown hair a mussed mess as usual. "Yep, it's me again. Do you feel like some company?"

"Don't even ask such a thing! I've just been sitting here wondering what to do with myself." Quickly she straightened the sheets around her waist, adjusted her bed a bit, and vainly wished she'd asked the morning nurse to help her smooth the hair under her *kapp*. Her hair most likely looked like a bird's nest. "Please, come in."

"Wondering what to do with yourself, hmm?" Kind hazel eyes looked her over and twinkled. "You must be feeling better."

"I am. Well, I am, a bit."

"That's good." He smiled as he shrugged off his tan canvas jacket and restlessly pushed back a portion of his straight brown hair that seemed to always want to cover one side of his forehead. "I see you've mastered the remote control. Are there any shows you like?"

Sorry that he'd guessed what she'd been doing, she pushed the black contraption farther away from her. Though he most likely wouldn't care that she'd been watching TV, she felt ashamed that she had done so. "Not so much." Wrinkling her nose, she added, "Much of what they talk about I don't understand."

"Because of the technology? I imagine information about cell phones and iMacs are hard to understand."

"Oh, no, I understand technology. I may not use it, but I'm fairly interested in all those gadgets. No, it's everything else that I find confusing. Yesterday I found three shows on ways to diet and exercise. Woman after woman talked about ways to change. I don't understand why so many people are displeased with the way God made them."

"That's because you see things a little more clearly than most. I'll bring you a book or some magazines next time I visit, if you'd like."

The fact that he talked about coming again made her happy. "*Danke.* I do like magazines, especially the gardening and cooking ones."

"I'll bring you as many as I can hold."

"I'd like that very much. I mean, if you don't mind."

"I don't. Not at all." As he took the chair next to her, Sam said, "I spoke with the nurses before I came in. They said you are doing better." Looking her over, he said, "Are you, really?"

"I am. Now I only have one needle in me, from this IV bag." She held up her hands for inspection, feeling so much freer than she'd felt since she'd arrived at the hospital.

"That is a good thing." He frowned at her arms, decorated with more than one or two purplish marks. "It's a shame you got so bruised, though."

"I'd rather have bruises than more bandages. They'll fade in time."

"Did the doctor tell you any more news?"

"Not anything of use. He reminded me of the fact that I'm going to have a difficult time walking around and doing my chores. He said the bones in my foot are going to take their time to heal." Remembering the conversation, she added, "First I am to be in a wheelchair. Then, if I'm very good, I might get to only have crutches for five weeks."

To her delight, Sam laughed. "I better warn Jonathan! He already says you hate to slow down. You'll be a dangerous woman in a wheelchair."

"Not so much. Besides, I imagine I'll be slow for quite a while, I'm afraid."

"That's a good thing."

"Maybe."

"It is. And, listen, you must promise to use that wheelchair as an excuse to be a lazybones."

"Perhaps—but that's not who I am—or who I want to be." Winnie tried hard to not think about why she even cared about what Sam thought of her. For the last few years, she'd practically given up on love. When she was a teen, the boys used to tease her because she was so skinny and tall. Later, other boys had complained about her outspoken ways. And though she'd learned to be a bit more patient and to curb her tongue as well, there often seemed to be other areas where she had felt lacking.

All of it had taken a toll on her confidence.

Samuel shifted, propping one brown suede boot on a metal rung of her fancy electronic bed. Quietly, he murmured, "So, who do you want to be?"

"Just myself, I suppose. That's enough, *jah*?" She hoped he wouldn't hear the lie in her voice. In truth, she wanted far more than the person she was. She wanted to be married and start her family. She wanted the things she'd always yearned for but never seemed to be able to grasp.

"It's definitely enough. You're *glikklich*, did you know that?"

"Why would you say I'm lucky?" His comment surprised her almost as much as his use of Pennsylvania Dutch.

Sam resituated himself, flopping an elbow up on a knee. Somehow he always managed to look completely relaxed—even in such a stark hospital room. "Me, I've never been that happy with just myself. I always have had too many goals, I suppose."

"Such as?"

"Oh, nothing worth mentioning right this minute. It would put you to sleep."

"You'd never put me to sleep."

When his eyebrows rose, she felt her cheeks heat and thought quickly to save herself from embarrassment. "I mean, I've been given so many medications, it's hard for me to sleep."

"That's to my benefit, hmm? Now I don't have to worry about keeping your attention."

When he flashed a grin, she smiled, too. Winnie tried to convince herself that the only reason she was smiling was because she wasn't sitting alone anymore. The job was fairly tough to do. Sam Miller conversed with the easiness of a person who was confident with himself and his world.

That confidence made her feel completely giddy and a bit off kilter. He looked at her the way she'd always hoped a man would. The way Malcolm, her pen pal in Indiana, never had.

*But he is not here to see you. He is here to check on you as a favor to his brother*, she reminded herself.

As the silence between them lengthened, she became more aware of how close he was sitting to her. Of how much she'd been thinking about him without meaning to.

Only a brisk ding from the nurses' station down the hall broke the spell. "You can tell me about your dreams. I'd find them interesting. What are some things you'd like to change?"

But Sam still looked uncomfortable. "Nothing today." Before she could respond, he spoke again. "Now, no more about me. I'm supposed to be asking you the questions."

Well, she could be stubborn, too. "I refuse to answer any more questions." Remembering a bit of advice her mother had once relayed to her,

Winnie said, "Tell me about your life with the English, Samuel."

Leaning back in his chair, he looked at her a little more closely. She met his gaze and felt a little spark of something special pass between them.

Awareness?

She knew what it was—it was the feeling she'd hoped to feel with boys as a teenager. It was the zing she'd ached to feel for Malcolm but never had. Now, here it was, unbidden and bursting with surprise, and there wasn't a thing she could do about it.

Oblivious to her thoughts, Sam shifted again. "There's not so much to tell." He shrugged. "You know most everything. I work at the agricultural college."

She was interested in more than just his occupation, but beggars couldn't be choosers. "Come now, Samuel, there's a lot to say about that job, I imagine. What do you do there?"

"This and that. I teach. Mentor students."

Oh, getting him to talk was like pulling teeth! "What do you talk to the students about?"

"Their futures." With measured words, he added, "English kids have so many options I think that sometimes they don't know what they want. I try and help them focus."

His statement caught her attention. In a way, she couldn't help but feel envious. Oh, she'd never had huge desires to accomplish great things. But it did sound intriguing to have so many opportunities at her fingertips. And to even have someone with experience to guide her, why that sounded mind-boggling. "Are you successful? Do they . . . focus?"

Samuel laughed, a deep, rich sound that floated through the air and lodged in her heart. "Sometimes. Not everyone's future is easy to figure out, you know."

"I imagine. What else do you do besides work with students?"

"I spend a lot of time in the fields and gardens, experimenting with soil composites and fertilizer." His voice warming, he said, "Lately, I've been trying to promote our Amish ways to everyone else. Too many people want to substitute science with what works. I don't always trust the results, you know?"

"Do people listen?"

"Sometimes. Organic produce is fairly popular right now. People are interested in our natural ways of insecticide and our practice of composting." Folding his hands around a knee, he said, "Just the other day, we studied how earthworms break down soil and help root expansion. Oh, sorry. I forget that not everyone is interested in worms and dirt."

"I am." But in spite of her best intentions, she yawned. "I mean, I'm interested in your take on things, especially with other people's interest in the Amish. Their curiosity makes me smile. So, our old ways are new now?"

Chuckling, he nodded. "That they are. But some would say that is how things always have been—people are adopting techniques that were always there, just forgotten."

"I've noticed that at my shop. I've met many people who now are appreciating the smooth lines and fine workmanship of master craftsmen."

"I'll have to visit your shop when you get better."

"It's not mine, of course, but I do enjoy working there."

"What else do you enjoy? Gardening?"

"I do. Not like you, but I do like getting my hands dirty and producing something. I'm not much of a person for cooking or sewing, but I do enjoy a day in the garden."

"So you garden and work at an antique shop."

"Yes. And you work and . . . do what?" she prompted, wanting to know more. Sam intrigued her, pure and simple.

A shadow fell over his eyes. "I work and read mostly. Hike and bike. Every now and then I watch a movie."

"I've only seen a few movies. One time we stayed in a hotel and my parents let us watch *Cinderella* on the television. I saw a few others when I went over to an English friend's home."

"Maybe I'll bring a movie for us to watch tomorrow."

"I'd like that, if you have the time." She took a chance. "That is, if you don't have a date or something."

He visibly started. "A date? No. I, um, don't date much."

"I'm surprised." Samuel Miller was a handsome man.

"You shouldn't be." A ruddy blush colored his cheeks. "I . . . I sometimes wonder how I fit in, if you want to know the truth. A lot of the women I meet are from different backgrounds. Sometimes I feel like I am speaking *Deutsch*, our views are so crisscrossed. They think my ways are old-fashioned and quaint."

"I heard some women don't even go to church."

"No, they don't. Some have far different values than I do. Even though I left the Amish, I don't think my heart did."

"That's a terrible place to be," she said softly. "I would imagine it would be hard to straddle two worlds."

"I'm not trying to straddle, just fit in. But I wouldn't say my path is 'terrible.' It's difficult, but it is the path I've chosen. I chose to leave the Amish in order to further my education. Because I chose to leave, I must also live with the consequences."

"But don't you wish things were easier?"

Samuel considered her question for a moment before shrugging. "Sometimes. But, Winnie, truthfully, I don't pray for things to become easier.

Instead I pray for patience. God never promised us an easy life, and I don't think I need an easy life— just one I can feel good about."

"I hear what you are sayin'. And you're right. Even in the Amish community, people have struggles." Taking a chance, Winnie dared to reveal a bit more about herself. "Last year, I wrote to a man for quite a time. I thought he and I might have a future one day. But when I went out to Indiana to visit him, I found we didn't suit each other after all."

"And you were disappointed?"

"I was. I . . . I never told my family, but I knew as soon as I saw Malcolm that I'd never fall in love with him. There was nothing about him that struck my fancy. But I tried to pretend there was a possibility." Winnie felt her cheeks heat. At the moment, she would have given most anything to run out of the room. Never before had she admitted how hard she'd tried to make things work with Malcolm. It had been difficult, indeed. "After three weeks, I gave up."

"Three weeks is a long time to give someone!"

"It was. But I was so determined to make something happen." She shook her head. "In the end, it was no good. It was like trying to put a round knob in a square hole."

"I hope one day you find your match."

"*Danke.* I hope you will one day find your match, too."

"If we're lucky, we'll take that big step one day. I just hope when we do, the path won't be too painful."

"We'll hope and pray." Winnie forced herself to look anywhere but directly at him. She was afraid if she met his gaze, he'd see what she was trying so hard to conceal. Pointing to her feet, she grinned. "I've been learning that sometimes even when our paths aren't always easy, one survives. And sometimes, it is worth all the hardship."

"That's good advice." His lips twitched. "As long as it doesn't involve a broken foot."

"I'll let you know if my foot's pain is worth it." She blinked as he laughed. And finally, gave in to the pull that was happening between them. An invisible, tenuous bond held them together. She felt it as much as she had felt the instinctive knowledge that Malcolm would never be for her.

For a split second, she spied hope and a yearning that matched the feelings in her heart.

Winnie forgot she was sitting in a hospital bed with needles and bandages over her. She forgot how unhappy she'd been. How much she'd wished things would change and that she be given an opportunity to do something new with her life.

All she seemed to be able to think about was the man sitting next to her. How his hair was streaked with gold from hours in the sun. How his shoulders and arms looked like they could hold the biggest load of wood with ease. She noticed the calluses on his fingers, and the lines around his eyes that had nothing to do with age and everything to do with laughing and living.

But even more importantly, she noticed the things that had nothing to do with looks. His sun-streaked hair hinted of his love of the outdoors. The calluses and muscles showed he wasn't afraid to carry burdens. The lines on his face proved he wasn't afraid to live.

But as her fancies settled down, Winnie slid back to reality with a thump. He wasn't Amish. It was too late for both of them. It was now too late to even dream.

Clearing her throat, she said, "I'll look forward to those magazines and a book. Thank you again for offering to bring some reading material."

His expression clearing, Samuel nodded as he stood up. "Like I said, it is no trouble. I'll bring them by tomorrow. And that movie I promised?"

"I would enjoy that. A special treat, indeed."

Backing out of the room, he nodded. "I'll go, then."

"Yes. I'll see you tomorrow. Goodbye, Sam."

When the door closed and the room felt too big, Winnie pretended it was only her foot that was hurting.

# Chapter 5

David had never meant to start the fire. All he'd been doing was trying his hardest to make smoke rings. He and two other boys had seen some English teenagers making perfect circles in the air outside the Brown Dog Café. When David had seen how impressed his friends had been, he'd become determined to make them, too.

They were much harder to make than he'd thought.

That night, well, he'd been so intent on spying those rings in the moonlight, he hadn't realized that he hadn't been extinguishing the cigarettes like he should.

At least, he supposed that was what had happened.

But once that first spark flickered, then flashed into flames, he'd hardly had time to do anything but back away in a panic—the blaze got so big so quickly.

But still, even then, he'd stayed nearby. After all, he knew he was at fault. The right thing to do would be to alert the Lundys and help get all the animals out of the barn.

But all he could think about was what his *daed* would do when he found out.

When he heard Jonathan Lundy's shout and the frightened shrieks of the horses, he'd felt relief. Jonathan would take care of everything. And so he ran farther into the shadows. He wanted to help. Honestly, he wanted to do whatever he could, but it was surely too late.

Besides, it seemed as if his feet were running faster than his mind could work. Like lightning, he'd run across the back fields, the tall grasses whipping against his knees like miniature reminders.

When he got home, his *daed*'s kerosene lamp glowed from the window of his parents' bedroom. He'd let himself in just as he heard the familiar thump, thump of his father's thick-soled shoes echoing through the darkness. He knew what his father was going to do—he was going to ride out to the Lundys' and give assistance. Most likely, his well-honed sixth sense had alerted him to a fire nearby.

That's what his father always did—the right thing. He'd never had patience for people who didn't follow rules. He didn't believe in gray areas. No, things were stark in his father's world. Either a person was right or wrong. And if someone was wrong, that was usually unforgivable.

He'd hardly had time to hide in the shadows before his father had mounted their mare and rushed to the farm.

And then the next morning, when he heard Winnie was in the hospital and that the whole barn was ruined, it was too late to say a word.

What was done was done.

How could he confess what he'd done? No one would understand his reasonings anyway. He hadn't meant to set the fire. He hadn't meant to run and hide. But he had. He didn't understand why things had happened.

Now he couldn't help but wonder if this was God's way of punishing him for smoking.

He'd decided right then and there never to smoke again. He hid his last carton and lighter from sight. When the time was right, he'd take it into town and toss it in a trash can. He didn't dare dispose of anything around the farm. He was too afraid.

But now David couldn't sleep. Something told him that things still weren't right. They would never be until he admitted all his wrongs.

But every time he thought of the expression on his parents' face, he dared not say a word.

Truthfully, there was little he could do now. What was done was done. Now he just had to hope and pray that no one would ever find out. If his father ever discovered the truth, he'd be horribly angry. So angry David was afraid to tell him.

But what he did still shamed him.


"Thank you all for coming. I know I need your help to make these difficult decisions," Jonathan began, looking toward Henry Brenneman and his father, John, Eli Miller, and Marvin Kropfs, the bishop of their church. "I spoke with the fire marshal and he assured me that their investigation is complete. They've called the fire an accidental one, that was set by a stray cigarette."

The other men looked at each other in consternation. The bishop's expression hardly flickered—it was almost like he hadn't heard a thing.

But that was his usual way of listening—impassive. Stoic.

Jonathan wondered what was going through their minds. He'd seated them all at the dining room table, where they could see each other equally around the oval and take notes if needed. But as the moments passed, Jonathan began to doubt his instincts. Maybe he should have asked Bishop Kropfs for a more formal meeting at another location?

Maybe he should have just said nothing and waited for someone else to bring things up?

Finally Bishop Kropfs spoke. "Jonathan, if the police and fire investigators said their work is over, does that mean they no longer need to come nosing around here?"

"I believe so. We can rebuild and move on." Quietly, he added, "It doesn't look as if someone was meaning to do harm . . ." His voice drifted off. He wanted to give whoever had done the damage the benefit of the doubt. He wanted to concentrate on moving forward instead of looking backward, but the positive, optimistic words felt stuck in his throat.

The truth was, he felt bitter and angry inside. He

wanted retribution. He wanted someone to be punished for the destruction and danger caused.

"Accidents happen, Jonathan," the bishop said with a shrug, looking at Henry's father meaningfully. "Perhaps it was God's will."

Jonathan knew what that shared look meant—the two older men thought he was acting a little too rash and foolishly.

Maybe he was.

But, for the life of him, Jonathan couldn't think of a single reason why the good Lord would have wanted his barn to burn to the ground.

Though, of course, it wasn't his place to question the Almighty. But still, the Lord had given him a mind, too, and he was intent on using it. "I realize that the Lord has His ways, but there are signs that it might have been someone in our community who set the fire. Accident or not, the fire was a terrible thing."

"We were right lucky Winnie wasna hurt worse."

"Only by the grace of God did we get the animals out and Winnie to safety," Jonathan agreed. "However, now I find myself unable to sleep. I think about Katie and Mary and Hannah. What would have happened if my girls had been here? What if the fire had spread more than it did? I could have lost my house." Haltingly, he added, "I could have lost my girls."

Henry whistled low. "But you didn't. Come now, *freind*. Don't dwell on what didn't happen."

"I'm having trouble only looking at the bright side. Too much was in danger."

A new awareness entered John Brenneman's expression. "I hear what you are saying . . . I, too, have been plagued by 'what-ifs.' After all, I, too, have a daughter who could've been caught in the fire. But . . . that doesn't change the fact that Winnie is all right, your animals are okay, the girls and Katie are unharmed, and your house is fine. We shouldn't go borrowing trouble."

Frustrated by the other men's inability to read his mind, Jonathan shook his head. "John, you are right, but that is not what concerns me. See, I'm wondering what I should do about the culprit. Should I give the police permission to try and figure out who started the blaze, or should I just let the investigation fall and move on?"

Bishop Kropfs sipped from his coffee, and obviously finding it cold, frowned and pushed it away. "Cigarettes are not against the law. How could anyone even begin to figure out who did such a thing? That investigation sounds impossible."

John nodded as well. "Monitoring the English is not something we should be worried about. Besides, who could it be? I couldn't help with any ideas. I know many of the English, but not their habits."

Jonathan sighed. Obviously, he was going to have no choice but to share all of his worries. "Katie suggested that it's more likely to be an Amish teen. I think she might have a point."

"C-certainly not," the bishop stammered. "No member of our group would do such a thing."

As the other men looked just as horrified, Jonathan hastened to explain himself. "While at first I was shocked, now the idea makes more sense to me. My place is familiar to everyone in our community—but not to outsiders. After all, there's no reason for an *Englischer* to be sneaking around my land, just to have a smoke. There're many other places that would be far more convenient."

"English teens still do sneak around, though. Even English parents don't smile upon teenagers doing such things." John waved a hand. "Most likely there was beer or wine or something hidden in your barn, too. Or, it could have been a pair of teens." He raised his brows. "Put that way, your barn would be a far sight better spot to play around in than a parked car."

Henry chuckled. "*Daed,* the things you say. Sometimes you still surprise me."

"I'm old but not *deerich,*" John replied with a wink.

Bishop Kropfs chuckled. "No, you have never been a foolish man, John."

Choosing his words carefully, Jonathan said, "While I agree that my barn is a secluded spot, I still don't think it is a likely place for English teens. And, the police didn't find any evidence of liquor bottles or cans. I think we need to consider the idea that it was one of our members. An Amish child doesn't have as many options for foolishness. It really does make the most sense."

"I'm afraid I have to agree," Eli said, looking a bit worried. "It would be wrong to not imagine that someone in our order made a terrible mistake the other night. We all remember feeling our oats, so to speak."

"Even if it was an Amish teen—which I doubt— I'm not sure why you called us together," the bishop said.

Jonathan's throat went dry. Without so much as raising his voice, it was obvious that their bishop was not pleased with the proceedings or the thread of conversation. Katie's dad was starting to look uncomfortable, too.

Slowly, he looked each man in the eye and finally got around to the real reason he'd sought their company. "The fact that it could have been a member of our community concerns me greatly. If a teenager did cause such an accident, it bothers me that he or she hasn't come forward and admitted his responsibility."

"That is troublesome," John murmured.

It was finally time to admit the thing that was bothering him the most, even if it didn't make him feel proud. "I, personally, don't know if I'll be able to move forward without knowing who did this."

The bishop peered at Jonathan over his half-moon spectacles. "You could, with God's help."

John Brenneman chimed in. "If it was an accident, it shouldn't matter who caused the damage."

"*Jah.* You need to forgive, Jonathan," the bishop muttered, his voice laced with impatience. "You need to *bayda*, to pray and ask for guidance."

Jonathan struggled to keep his expression as neutral as the others'. At least, thankfully, Eli and Henry weren't saying too much. It would be even harder if the both of them were feeling the same way.

He chose his next words with care. "I would like to forgive whoever trespassed on my land and did so much damage. But how can I if the person responsible hasn't accepted any blame? If the person hasn't even asked for forgiveness?" Frustrated with the whole situation, he pushed back his chair and braced his hands on the thick oak tabletop. "Someone put everything I love in harm's way and hasn't even bothered to step forward. It eats me up inside."

"It would bother me, too," Henry said.

"I'm afraid I will not give my blessing to your investigation, Jonathan. What's done is done." The bishop pushed back his chair and looked ready to leave.

Every time Jonathan closed his eyes, he felt as if the fire was ablaze once again. The all-encompassing rage and terror of those moments, when he wasn't sure if Winnie was all right. His fear that all the animals would burn to death. In his heart, he knew he would never be able to accept the situation and put it behind him without answers.

Even if it went against the basic tenets of their beliefs.

After a lengthy pause, the bishop proclaimed, "I suggest we accept that we might never know who trespassed on the property and move on. Whoever did this will surely be feeling guilt, mark my words. And, of course, judgment is not ours to give, but rather our maker's."

The other men nodded. Reluctantly, Jonathan did as well, but the decision didn't sit well with him. He knew forgiveness was one of the tenets of their community. But still, he found he could not simply accept the fact that someone had trespassed, accidentally burned down his property, and almost killed his family and then got away.

Long after the men left, Jonathan stood outside and stared at the remains of the barn. Plain and simply, he was angry about the damage. He still felt as if a frog was in his throat every time he thought about what could have happened to his sister.

And while he could accept an accident, he surely didn't know if he could accept a lie for the rest of his life. As of now, he knew every time he spied a teen looking sheepish or secretive, he would blame him.

And surely, that wasn't right either, now was it?

"Jonathan, you're still out here?" Katie asked as

she walked out to stand beside him. Staring at the charred remains of the building, she folded her arms over her chest. "Are you planning to join us inside anytime soon?"

"Maybe." He would go inside if he could shake the anger and sense of helplessness that coursed through him every time he glanced at the remains of the barn. Being around his daughters while filled with such bitterness wouldn't be good at all.

"Maybe, hmm?" Instead of sounding perturbed, Katie just seemed amused. "I'll tell Hannah that, then. I'm sure she'll understand that her *daed* doesn't know when he's going to tell her *gud naught.*"

In what had become a habit, Jonathan reached for her hand. Very sweetly, she slipped hers in his and held on tight. As always, her palm felt cool and smooth and reassuring. So ladylike and feminine, but strong, too.

Remembering how hard it used to be for him to trust, he took a chance. "I'm having a time accepting the bishop's decision."

"What was it?"

"We're supposed to simply rebuild and let the Lord take care of the rest. Katie, I don't know if I can do that."

Instead of replying immediately, she released his hand and walked over to the burnt remains of the barn. With a loving hand, she ran a finger over one of the few planks that was completely whole. "This has been a special place, hasn't it?"

"What do you mean?"

She turned to him. "Oh, Jonathan, I know it has to bring back memories of your father, and your grandfather, too." She raised a brow. "Doesn't it?"

"Some." A lump formed in his throat as he thought of all he'd lost in a few hours' time. Saddles were gone. His father's finely honed bridle. His grandfather's ax.

No, he hadn't lost memories, but he had lost the tangible evidence that people important to him had existed. He'd lost items close to his heart—items he'd one day wanted to hand on to his daughters or a future son.

The barn's destruction made him feel loss similar to when his father passed away, after his long battle with cancer.

Picking up a charred board, Katie examined the dark shadows marking the wood before easily breaking it in half. Blackened splinters sprinkled the ground and her skirts right before she loosened her grip and let the pieces fall to the ground. "I also see reminders of how I used to feel." She turned to him, her vibrant blue eyes seeking his. "If it was an Amish teen who did this, then he or she must be feeling fairly terrible. I, personally, felt guilt for years for the lies I once told to both my English friends and my family."

"What are you sayin'? That you would have liked to have been caught?"

"I'm not certain." She shrugged. "But I do know that while we can break the past and try our best to toss it from our life, it's not always that easy." With a small smile, Katie opened her hands, revealing black stains on her fingertips. "Even after pushing away the damage, we're still marked."

"Yes, but your hands can be washed."

"It's not as easy to remove tough stains as one might think, Jonathan." Stepping toward him again, Katie murmured, "For both your sake and the teen's I am glad you are not going to simply drop what happened."

"And if we don't find anything right away?"

"I don't want to go against the elders' wishes, but maybe it wouldn't be a bad thing to do a little guessing and questioning on your own. It's your right, after all. This was your property."

"I don't want to go against the Bishop."

"I wouldn't want you to. But I don't want to see you miserable either. I think it might be a mistake to assume that just because there is fresh wood in this place that the past can be erased."

"I'll think on that." There was so much to think about, his head was spinning.

"In the meantime, perhaps it is time to come inside? There're two girls who would love to spend some time with you."

He took her hand again and held it firmly as they walked away from the burned remains. Away from the doubts to the certainty of all that he had . . . a wife and two lovely daughters. A home and a place to go home to. That, indeed, gave him comfort.

# Chapter 6

"So, tomorrow is the big day, right?" Sam asked when he entered Winnie's hospital room. For once, he actually looked like he was coming from his job at the college. He held a thick leather satchel in his right hand and had on a blazer.

"Yes. I am going home tomorrow. I am terribly anxious to leave." Gesturing toward his fancy jacket, she said, "I guess you've been at work?"

"Yep." He made a face. "I had one meeting after the other. First with the department chair, then with a couple of prospective students who wanted to know more about the agriculture program. That's why I couldn't stay too long yesterday. I had a lot to prepare for."

"I understood." She'd needed that time to herself anyway. She'd spent hours thinking about their relationship, struggling to remind herself that there was little between them other than a matter of convenience for a short time. Sam lived and worked near the hospital. She, Winnie, had just happened to be nearby for a time. After tomorrow, their friendship would fade away again, just like it had years before.

That wasn't a bad thing. No, it was just how things were.

"I know you are a busy man."

"I hope you believed me when I said I had a lot

of work to do. I really couldn't get out of it."

She didn't appreciate his tone. "I'm not a child, Samuel. Nor backward." He winced but she couldn't help but let him hear the displeasure in her voice. "I might not have gone to work in a college, but I still can understand responsibilities."

"I didn't mean to act as if you didn't."

Now she felt self-conscious. "I'm sorry. Sometimes my tongue runs away with me."

"Can we call a truce? I brought you something." He held up a flat plastic box.

Winnie played along. "Now what might that be?"

He smiled broadly. "It's a movie. *Singin' in the Rain.*"

"*Singin' in the Rain*? I've never heard of such a thing. Most times we try to dodge the rain, not sing in it."

Looking almost boyish, Samuel popped open the box, then pulled out a silver disc. "You, Winnie Lundy, are in for a treat. People say that *Singin' in the Rain* is the best musical of all time."

She wasn't even sure what exactly a musical was. But still, seeing a movie was indeed a treat, and one she would likely be grateful for in the years to come. "Plug it in, then."

He chuckled. "Say, play the movie, Samuel."

She obediently complied. "Play, Samuel."

Just as he inserted the disc into the player, Nurse Brenda came in with a bowl of popcorn. "Here's your movie treat," she said, beaming.

"Oh, *danke*! I do love popcorn!"

"Have a good time, you two," the nurse said as she walked back out the door.

Holding the bowl in her lap, Winnie smiled. "That was nice of her."

"It was. I asked her to pop up some in the microwave for us. Can't watch a movie without that."

Winnie couldn't help but stare at the contents in the bowl with a new distrust. "I've never had microwave popcorn. Is it safe?"

Humor filled his hazel eyes. "As safe as watching a movie, Winnie."

And with that, he pressed play, sat in the chair next to her, and grabbed a handful of popcorn just as a tall man in funny old-fashioned clothes started talking about being a movie star.

Winnie couldn't help it, she was enchanted. She'd only seen a few other movies, and those had been with an English friend back when she was eight. Never had she seen a movie with such singing and dancing!

She found herself munching the popcorn and sharing smile after smile with Sam, laughing at the blonde's voice. Every so often, she'd ask Samuel a question about the movie's plot or characters. He answered each one like they weren't silly at all.

And when their hands touched while grabbing a handful of popcorn, Winnie pretended not to notice how much even such a simple touch affected her.

All she knew, was that long after Gene Kelly and Debbie Reynolds looked into each other's eyes and kissed, long after Sam had put the movie back in the case and departed, long after the smell of popcorn was replaced by the scent of antiseptic . . . she still remembered exactly what it had felt like to be completely happy in Samuel Miller's company.

"I am very grateful for all of your help these last few days," Winnie said to Brenda the following morning. "I have much appreciated all you've done for me."

"It was no bother."

"I'm sure it was. When I first got here, I was in sad shape."

"You certainly are doing much better now, I'm pleased to say." Brenda briskly moved around the room in her squeaky sparkling white tennis shoes, picking up cards and rearranging items quickly and efficiently. "I've liked getting to know you and learning more about your kind. You're my first Amish patient, you know."

Winnie would have taken a bit of exception to Brenda's phrasing of "her kind" except that now she knew Brenda well enough to understand what she meant. During the five years that she'd worked at the hospital, Brenda had told her about patients from many different countries that visited. She loved learning about different cultures and traditions.

As Brenda watched Winnie carefully smooth her dress's fabric around her waist, she frowned. "Don't these pins that hold your dress together ever stick you?"

Winnie chuckled at the question. "Not yet. You learn as a young girl to fasten them carefully."

"Your hair looks all neat and tidy."

"I'm glad of that. It's felt like a mess of tangles."

"It's pretty. Why, it's the silkiest hair I've ever braided. Long, too."

"I told you we don't cut our hair."

"Well, you look fetching now that it's neat and tidy under your *kapp*."

"Brenda, you sound almost Amish!"

*"Danke!"*

"Oh, Brenda, I will miss you." Impulsively, Winnie hugged her nurse, who looked at first taken aback by the burst of emotion, then a little teary-eyed.

"Don't forget to take care of yourself, you hear? The burns are out of the danger zone, but the skin will be tender." Waving a finger, she added, "And go easy on that foot. There's a big difference between sitting around here and hopping around at home."

"I don't think I could get much done, even if I wanted to." Gingerly, she got into the wheelchair the orderly held for her. Brenda was about to hand over her bag full of belongings when Sam and Eli bolted through the door.

"Are we late, Win?" Eli asked, his face red and splotchy.

"Almost. What took you two so long?"

Sam held up a hand. "Don't let him lay a bit of this blame on me. I was at his house early this morning but he wasn't ready."

"Cow has colic."

Brenda wrinkled her nose. "You're talking about a real cow, right? Like one that says 'moo'?"

Instead of looking abashed, Eli seemed anxious to share his story. "Oh, you bet. She's better now, but it was touch and go for a time."

"She's a stubborn heifer, that's for sure." Sam chuckled. "She's worse than a child about taking her medicine."

Eli grimaced. "Far worse. She kept stomping her hooves and bellowing every time Caleb ventured near." Sharing a look with his brother, he added, "Though now that I think about it, I don't think Caleb was too sad about that."

"He wouldn't be," Sam stated. "He's a master of dodging chores."

"Like you would know," Eli retorted.

Winnie held a hand up in protest. "Stop, you two! You're here now, so that's all that matters."

"That's right," Brenda added with a grin. "All that matters is you're here for Winnie's big departure."

"*Jah*, and I'm ready, too."

To her surprise, Sam crouched right down next to

85

her, bringing with him a sharp, clean, heady scent that she couldn't ignore. "You look ready. It's good we didn't wait a moment longer."

She had no desire to look anywhere but at him. Feeling like a teenager, especially with Brenda watching with interest, she fought off the flutter of nerves that were threatening her composure. "Yes. I would have flown the coop and you two would have had to search the countryside for me."

"I don't think you would've gotten very far, hopping on one foot." Eli frowned at his brother. "Get up, Samuel. You're blocking everyone's way."

Slowly, Sam stood up. Then, their procession started forward. The orderly pushing her, Brenda walking by her side, Eli now holding her belongings . . . and Samuel keeping everyone company.

Funny how he seemed to be the only person she was aware of.

Winnie looked from Eli to Sam and tried to pretend that one of them didn't affect her like Sam did. But the truth was that every time Sam Miller was in her presence, there seemed to not be enough air in the room. Her breath ran short, and her pulse raced a bit more than usual.

Brenda winked her way. "Sam and Eli, I best remind you both that Winnie here needs to be treated like a lady of leisure."

"I'll make sure of it," Sam said.

"What's a lady of leisure?" Eli muttered.

"A woman who sits around a lot," Sam explained.

"Ah."

As the orderly and Brenda bantered back and forth, Winnie met Sam's gaze. "Thanks for driving me home today."

"It's no problem. I am sorry I'm late."

"You're not. I just got released."

Eli grunted. "There's a lot of traffic today, Win. It's going to be quite a while before we're back home again."

She looked Sam's way as they continued their way down the hall, its pungent antiseptic scent almost making her eyes water. "I hope we won't ruin your whole day?"

"You won't. I decided to take a few days off from school. I have some vacation days coming."

Eli looked at his older brother fondly. "He's going to help with the plowing and planting."

"Really?" Winnie looked from one brother to the other. Since she'd known the Millers, she'd never known Eli to ever ask for help or for Sam to come out and assist. "Is that the only reason?"

"Eli also explained how Jonathan and Henry sometimes lend a hand, but there won't be time with the Lundy barn needing to be rebuilt. And, well, Jonathan also told me that you've got a follow-up appointment in a few days' time. When Katie said she was going to hire a sitter and a driver to accompany you, I thought I'd just stay out your way and take you then."

"That's mighty nice of you. A most generous use of your vacation."

"It's what I want to do." He sighed. "Plus, well, Caleb's been around less than usual. It's starting to be that no one can count on him for anything. Eli told me that last night Caleb went out and didn't show up until almost midnight. I'm beginning to really regret my parents' long trip north, especially since it's during Caleb's *rumspringa*. He doesn't always want to listen to his brothers."

"That will pass soon, I imagine."

Winnie felt a bubble burst inside of her. For a moment, there, she'd been sure Sam was staying nearby to see her. But, surely, his reasons were far better. After all, he'd left their community. She needed to remember that.

# Chapter 7

"And then, of course, McClusky told everyone to behave themselves in his store. That caused a commotion, I tell ya," Eli continued as Sam drove the three of them along the narrow, hilly lanes that made up the Amish community. After checking Winnie out from the hospital, they'd gone through a drive-thru for burgers, then started for the Lundy farm. And along the way, Eli had become a chatterbox, relaying neighborhood news with the exuberance of a gossipy maiden aunt.

"You know how McClusky is," Eli said, continuing. "Not much happens around here that he doesn't know about."

"Uh-huh." As Sam slowly curved the steering wheel right on to an unmarked street, he tried to remember who McClusky even was. But there was no use asking Eli to clarify things. Ever since they'd left the city and driven southwest toward the Amish communities, he'd become determined to fill Sam in on every momentous—and not so momentous—occasion that had happened over the last six months.

There'd been quite a lot of occasions. Sam appreciated the update. Truly, he cared about the people in this area very much but, nevertheless, felt removed, as if the people Eli were speaking of were characters in a story.

And though he'd been the one to leave, Sam felt uncomfortable about it. And a little guilty. He wasn't part of the Amish community anymore. This place was based on close family ties and sacrifices. Their parents both worked hard to see all their children's physical and emotional needs met. He felt selfish to have only thought of himself over the past couple of years.

"Don't forget to turn left at the Johnsons' place," Eli cautioned. "It's the house with the three flowering pear trees, Samuel."

Quickly Sam tapped the breaks and veered left. When Eli started up again about the day the trees were planted, Sam peeked in the rearview mirror.

Winnie was still sleeping. Her head listed to one side, her lips slightly parted. She looked peaceful.

For much of the drive, she'd dozed off and on. Sam couldn't help but glance her way every now and then. During his visits to her bedside, the two of them had begun to converse enough that he felt more comfortable with her than with any other woman of his acquaintance.

Winnie wasn't afraid to have opinions. She was smart, too, and he appreciated that. During their visits, she'd entertained him with stories about her friends and her new job at the antique shop. But unlike Eli's annoying chatter, Sam had been charmed. He enjoyed seeing the community through her eyes.

Likewise, she seemed to enjoy hearing stories of

his job and students, so much so that he wondered if she secretly wanted to continue her education.

He fought a yawn as Eli prattled on. Oh, he enjoyed hearing about the community. And, he dearly loved his older brother. But sometimes Eli simply forgot that his life was far different. It was like Eli assumed Sam could step back into the community as if he'd never left. It wasn't quite so easy. He'd changed. He was different—and in some ways maybe not for the better.

Instead of the lifelong friends and relatives in Eli's world, like Jonathan Lundy and Henry Brenneman, Sam's circle of friends was far more wide and varied. Though he got along with them fine, some of their beliefs challenged all the things he'd held dear.

In addition, while much of Eli's activities revolved around the family's needs, Sam's focus remained steadily on himself and his work. He spent hours a day working on research grants, student curriculums, and developing new and innovative methods for growing. Some were fascinating and challenged his brain in all the ways he'd hoped they would back when he dreamed of learning everything he possibly could. Other problems felt so insurmountable that he longed for dull, everyday conversations like the ones he was having.

None felt as personal as Eli's struggles with Caleb.

So why was his mind drifting?

As he downshifted and passed a black buggy, he found himself looking for the driver the same as Eli, just in case they found a familiar face.

Maybe he hadn't changed as much as he thought.

Ten minutes later, they pulled onto the Lundys' driveway. When Sam saw the destruction of the barn, his mouth went dry. Next to the pretty white-board house, the blackness of the building was startling.

He turned away from the damage just as Katie and her girls came out to greet them.

Groggily, Winnie sat up. "We're here already?"

"We are, sleepyhead," he said, his heart melting a bit at her half-closed eyes.

Eli pulled open Winnie's door and carefully helped her slide to the edge of her seat just as Katie rushed forward, pushing a wheelchair.

Winnie groaned. "I don't need that."

"Sure you do. We borrowed it from the Johnsons'."

Winnie tried not to let her pain show by biting the inside of her cheek. Their busy morning had jarred her body something fierce. Tender skin under bandages stung and her leg ached painfully. Moving around was sure different than sitting in a hospital bed all day!

Katie kissed her cheeks. "Winnie, I'm so glad you're back. It's been terribly quiet without you."

"Aunt Winnie, I lost a tooth!" Hannah exclaimed, impulsively reaching in and hugging her tight. Though she did her best to hide it, her whole body jumped in agony.

"Careful," Sam called out before Eli or Katie could say a word. "Your Aunt Winnie might be out of the hospital, but she isn't all better yet."

Hannah stepped back and blinked quickly, obviously fighting tears.

Mary, her little seven-year-old shoulders squared and resolute, stepped forward. "Here, Aunt Winnie. Let me help you."

"We'll be careful with her," Hannah murmured by Mary's side, her expression contrite.

Sam's cheeks colored. "I know. I, um, didn't mean to snap."

Though she was in a wheelchair, Winnie did her best to smooth things over. "Sam, it's fine. Girls, I missed you, too. Let's go on inside, shall we?"

Visibly gathering her wits, Katie nodded. "Yes, let's go in." With the girls' help, she pushed Winnie's chair along the smooth path toward the kitchen door, where no stairs interrupted their way. Sam picked up her bag and walked beside Winnie, his presence feeling as solid and comforting as it had in her hospital room.

When they entered the spotless kitchen, Winnie breathed in the appetizing aroma and smiled. "Katie, something smells mighty good."

"We made you soup, Winnie! Pronto Potato Soup," Hannah cried out. "There's vegetables in it that Mary cut up."

"That's my favorite. I'll look forward to tasting it."

"I've got your bed all ready for you, Winnie," Katie said. "Let's get you settled, then I'll bring you some tea. Or would you rather have soup right away?"

"I most certainly do not want to sit in bed. I'd fancy sitting in the *Sitzschtupp* and enjoying a nice cup of tea, if you don't mind."

"That's a *wonderbaar* idea! We can show you our quilt!" Mary said.

"I canna wait to see it."

Hannah pulled on her skirt. "We can show you our new fabric, too. It's yellow and purple. I love purple."

Winnie laughed. Oh, their enthusiasm was so good to see. She'd been so lonely in that sterile hospital room. "I love purple, too."

Katie frowned. "Perhaps it would be better not to wear your aunt out—"

"They're not wearing me out in the slightest. I welcome the company—the days were long at the hospital. Though I did have Samuel's visits to look forward to, I did get mighty lonely."

Katie raised her brows. "You looked forward to seeing him?"

"Well, yes." As Sam's cheeks flushed, Winnie

stumbled over her words. "I mean . . . I mean, he was so kind."

"I was glad to visit," Sam said. "Like I said, I work nearby."

Winnie rushed on. "Yesterday he brought me a movie to watch. And popcorn."

"Now isna that somethin'?" Katie murmured.

"I wanna go in the hospital now, too!" Mary exclaimed.

As Hannah chimed in, Winnie felt as if she was an awkward teen again. Sam looked uncomfortable and Katie looked as if she was doing all she could to mind her tongue—but had an awful lot to say. "Um, like I said, it's good to be home."

"Care for some tea before you get on your way, Samuel?" Katie asked.

"No, it's time I got goin'," Sam replied. "Eli and I were planning to talk about some growing techniques before we go out to the fields tomorrow. And Caleb is hopefully waitin', too." With a disgruntled expression, he added, "Eli says he hasn't been tending to his chores. I want to try and help persuade him."

When Katie and the girls left to get her some tea, Winnie found herself alone with Sam again. Now that they were back in familiar surroundings, she felt awkward and shy. Their differences seemed even more apparent than ever—as was the fact that things were changing.

There'd be no more movies or long talks about

their pasts and dreams to look forward to. She'd heal up and continue helping Katie and Jonathan, and Sam would go back to his life among the English.

Once again, she would be the old maid. The woman who'd found a future in a job instead of with a man and family of her own. She tried to tease to cover up the lump in her throat. "Thank you again for everything, Samuel. I'll always be grateful for your time."

"It was nothing. Perhaps I—"

"Samuel, you ready?"

"Yes." Sam took a step toward Eli, to where he was waiting by the door. "I suppose I'll see you in three days' time. When I drive you to the doctor."

"I'll look forward to it." She tried to keep her voice even, to not betray how happy his offer made her. "I mean, that is, if you're sure you can spare the time."

"I told you I could. I didn't lie."

"I know."

They shared a meaningful look. One of humor and of melancholy. Winnie felt that same curious jolt between the two of them. It was getting more and more of a struggle to pretend she didn't wish their circumstances were different.

Then Katie and Eli walked Sam away, out of her life.

Sam was just about to walk out the door when Katie stopped him. "Samuel, before you leave we would be grateful for your advice."

"About what?" Sam asked.

"Jonathan and Katie think it was most likely an Amish teen who set the blaze," Eli explained.

Katie continued. "The elders recommended Jonathan not do anything, but that's tough advice for him to follow. We might do a little investigating on our own." Looking somewhat guilty, she added, "I know we're not supposed to, but I feel that whoever did this needs to take responsibility. Winnie was badly injured."

Sam wasn't sure what he could do, but he had a feeling he'd feel just as strongly about wanting to do something—anything to feel like he was a part of the solution. "Any idea why someone would do such a thing?"

"No."

"Then how are you—"

"We might ask around a bit." She shrugged. "I'm hoping it merely was an accident. But even if it was, someone needs to apologize, don'tcha think?"

A strong sense of foreboding encompassed him. He'd been so wrapped up in his feelings for Winnie, he'd pushed aside the fact that the Lundys' barn had been set on fire. With care, he said, "Do you suspect anyone in particular?"

Katie nibbled on her bottom lip. "No one in particular . . ."

"Let's not mention any names. It would be foolish to make rash guesses," Eli inserted quickly.

Sam turned to him in surprise. What was that about? "Who are you thinking of, Eli?" Though they'd discussed Caleb's flighty ways, surely Eli now didn't imagine he was the guilty one?

"No one."

"I don't have anyone specific in mind," Katie said with a sigh. "Eli's right. I don't want to start pointing fingers. But . . ." Her voice drifted off.

"Something needs to be done," Sam finished.

Eli nodded. "*Jah*. Something surely needs to be done."

"It's too hard not knowing what happened," Katie added with a shrug. "And, well, there's always the worry that whoever started the fire could start another one."

A cool shadow passed through Sam. His brother knew something. Katie was worried more than she'd let on.

Was there more to all of this than he'd imagined?

Once again, Sam realized how many ways he'd cut himself off from the Amish community. He'd forgotten something that was basic to their way of life—they weren't backward or ignorant about the ways of the world. Instead, they *chose* not to adopt certain lifestyles of the current society.

They still had problems and gossips and differences with each other. Kids still didn't think ahead. People still made mistakes. This world wasn't completely sheltered and perfect—no, in some ways, it was just as filled with flaws as any other society.

He'd forgotten that.

After the men had gone, Winnie watched her sister-in-law slice a thick wedge of zucchini bread then carry it to where she waited. Still warm from the oven, the scent of the spiced treat made her mouth water. Oh, it was so nice to be home! "Katie, this looks wonderful *gut*."

"I thought you might be ready for something fresh and homemade," Katie replied with a smile. "How was the hospital food?"

"Not so bad. I wasn't especially hungry anyway."

"Your burns are healing?"

"Oh, yes. They're much better. My foot is, too. In fact, the doctor said he might have released me yesterday, but he wanted me to stay off my feet as much as possible for another day."

"We'll make sure you stay off of them now, too."

"That's not necessary. I'm tired, but otherwise fit. I can't wait to go to work, both here and at the store."

"We'll see what your brother has to say about that."

"Catch me up on all that I've missed. Do you really fear it was someone in our community who started the fire?"

"I don't know for sure, but it's my feeling. Nothing else makes much sense. The English have many places to smoke—it's not even looked down upon all that much. In our community, however, that would be a different story."

Winnie frowned. "I hate to start naming kids, but I can't but help to think of possible people."

Lowering her voice, Katie murmured, "I've even suspected Caleb Miller."

Winnie felt as if someone had punched her in the stomach. They suspected Sam and Eli's brother? "Really?"

"He lives within walking distance," Katie pointed out. "Not all the other kids do."

"I suppose." Caleb had changed some over the years—and it was clear both Eli and Sam were worried about him. But to imagine him responsible seemed farfetched. "I'm sure this has been bothering Jonathan as well," said Winnie. "Have you scheduled a raising?"

"Not yet. Actually, I think he's been wondering if it would be possible to do the barn raising near Henry and Anna's wedding in May. We'll have lots of friends and family in for that."

"Many hands will make the work better."

"He doesn't want to steal Anna's and Henry's attention, though."

Sipping her delicious tea, Winnie nodded. "I wouldn't want to do that neither. Anna's waited a mighty long time for this day."

Katie nodded, delicately nibbling on her bread. "She has. She never said a word, but I got the feeling she was disappointed that Jonathan and I got married so quickly, even though everyone knew she had to do things in her own time." Wiping a crumb from her skirt, she looked to Winnie. "So, are you going to tell me about Samuel?"

"There's not much to tell."

"I think maybe there is." Grabbing a cloth, she smoothed it over the fine wood of the oak table. "I've seen you sneak a peek at him a time or two."

Her sister-in-law's statement embarrassed her. "I look at everyone, Katie."

Katie stopped dusting and frowned. "Don't get your feathers ruffled. I'm just stating what I've seen. Though Samuel is six years older, I recall that more than one girl was taken with him when we were all in the same schoolhouse."

Winnie remembered that, too. Just as she remembered how confused she'd felt when she'd learned that he wanted to move away from all of them. "Now it doesna matter what I think or what I notice. He's not one of us anymore, Katie. That's all that matters."

"That's true. Yet . . . it is a shame, though."

"Yes." Winnie wasn't ready to share her thoughts, but they were there, perched on the edge of her tongue, plain as day.

Looking her over, Katie narrowed her eyes. "I

101

think there was something between you two. A spark."

Winnie knew there was. She felt lit up like a lightning bug whenever he was nearby. But that didn't make her reality any different. He was not for her, and couldn't be.

And she was so tired of disappointment. For whatever reasons, she'd never been drawn to any of the men in her order. And her visit with Malcolm had only made her dreams for love and marriage seem unattainable. Malcolm had been so self-centered and full of himself. They'd have whole conversations about his family, his goals, and his dreams . . . and never once would he ever consider that she might want something, too.

Now, of course, she'd become attracted to the absolute wrong person. If she didn't stop day-dreaming about Samuel Miller, all she'd be doing would be setting herself up for a good cry. Again.

# Chapter 8

"Where've you been, David?" Caleb Miller asked as he raced to catch up.

David shrugged. "Around."

"Not very around." Caleb huffed a bit as they ran down a slope near the back of the Lundys' land toward Wishing Well Lake. "You weren't at McClusky's on Saturday or with everyone at the Brown Dog on Friday night."

"I've had chores and stuff," David said, hoping that would explain away his hands. They still looked raw and hurt. He'd taken to dodging most everyone who would notice, not wanting to risk giving an explanation.

But Caleb had been persistent and hard to resist. Since the weather was especially warm, they'd both decided to go fishing, and maybe even take a dip in the lake. Their chores were done, the sky was robin's egg blue, and they had three hours until twilight, when it would be time to rush home for dinner and to feed the animals.

After they hopped a freshly painted fence and walked past a group of dairy cows, Caleb added, "I looked for you at Sunday's singing."

He bent his head down so his friend wouldn't realize how much his words affected him. He didn't have many friends, and if it wasn't for Caleb, most likely no one would have noticed

103

him missing. "I just didn't feel like goin'."

As was his way, Caleb accepted the reason without thinking about it twice. "Well, you sure missed a lot of talk."

"What about?"

"The Lundys' barn, of course."

He clenched his hands, glad Caleb wasn't looking at them. "What are people saying?"

Caleb didn't glance at him as he pushed aside a clump of long grass and led the way to the banks of the lake. "No one is any closer to figuring out who started the fire, but Jonathan's going to try and figure out who did it."

"Why?" he asked in a rush. "It was an accident."

Caleb stopped and looked his way. "Why would you say that?"

"I don't know. I mean, I thought that's what everyone was saying."

Caleb pulled out his fishing pole and opened up a jar filled with a good dozen night crawlers. "You're right. The fire inspector said arson is usually done a different way. Anyway, there're rumors that Jonathan Lundy might be going against Bishop Kropfs's wishes. No one knows what to think about that." After a good long pause, he said, "It's all kind of scary soundin', don'tcha think?"

He was so scared he thought he'd start crying like a baby. No one went against the bishop. Well, no one he'd ever heard of. "Why . . . why do ya think Jonathan is so determined?"

"My brothers were talking about it last night. I stood in the next room and listened. Basically, Sam and Eli say that Jonathan can't forgive the people who did this because they won't admit their mistakes." As if Caleb had just been talking about his math facts, he shrugged and pushed over the jar of night crawlers. "Take one and bait your hook. We ain't got all day, you know."

Dutifully, he pulled out a thick worm, stuck it on the hook, then cast off. "You know, maybe whoever started the fire never meant to do it."

Caleb rolled his eyes. "Of course the person had a reason."

"It could have just been an accident."

"Yeah, but if it was an accident, whoever did it would have admitted to it, don'tcha think? Jonathan Lundy would've gotten mad, but the person would have been forgiven."

"Sometimes it's not that easy."

"You're making it a whole lot harder than it has to be. It's our way to forgive—even if saying it and hearing it ain't easy."

"But—"

Caleb screwed up his face. "David, why are you quarreling about this? Whose side are you on anyway?"

"No one's. I'm . . . I'm just surprised someone would go against the bishop's wishes, that's all. My father says we're always supposed to mind our elders."

"Even when they're wrong?"

Especially when they're wrong. That's what faith was, right? But, as usual, he didn't say anything. He didn't dare go against Caleb—not when Caleb was his only good friend.

And, well, everyone liked Caleb Miller. If David got on his bad side, life would be even harder. "Never mind. Let's just fish, Caleb."

"Yeah. Sure."

Only the thought of hooking a big fish, big enough for Caleb to tell others about, gave David hope. That and the thought of how good fried catfish would be at supper.

"Just a little bit farther now," Henry Brenneman whispered in Anna's ear. "Careful now, mind the rock."

"Mind the rock! Oh, now that's quite a phrase for you to be saying, especially since I can't see a thing at the moment." Chills raced through her as he chuckled low and sweet against the nape of her neck.

Reaching out behind her, Anna reached for his hand. When his capable fingers curved around hers, she held fast. "It wasna necessary to blindfold me, you know. I would have gone wherever you wanted to guide me."

"I think differently."

She smiled even though she couldn't see his shining eyes. But even blindfolded, Anna knew he was pleased as punch. All morning he'd been staying close by her side. After they served guests, he'd invented a half-dozen reasons to stay in the kitchen far longer than normal. Why, he'd even helped her shake out the entryway rugs, something that he usually never ceased to avoid. Henry wasn't one for dust flying in his face. "So where are we going? And what is the occasion, please?"

"If I told you, it wouldn't be a surprise."

"Exactly!"

"Not one more word. Settle down, Anna. Just a few more steps. Trust me."

She did. She trusted Henry like no one else. With that in mind, she stopped fussing and put her hands in his and trusted.

Still holding one hand and taking comfort in the other that rested on her shoulder, Anna trudged on. Oh, the ground had never felt so rocky and difficult! Though her feet were encased in sturdy shoes, she still felt off kilter.

"Stop."

"Blindfold off now?"

Instead of replying right away, he merely slipped his fingers around the cloth and loosened the knot behind her head. "What do you see?" he whispered, his mouth close to her neck.

She blinked several times to allow her eyes to adjust. And then she noticed the stakes on the ground. "Is this for our home?"

"It is." Eagerly, he pulled her along, showing her where their bedroom, kitchen, and family rooms would be. When he slowed to a stop, he stomped his foot. "And this will be our front porch. Anna, within a year, we'll be greeting the morning sun from this spot."

She turned in a circle and then turned again, this time spinning fast enough that the air flew up under her skirts and belled them out. She giggled at the thought of behaving like a schoolgirl. But that's what she felt like! Free and in love and happy. "It looks perfect, Henry."

Suddenly the emotion of all they'd been through caught up with her. "We're so blessed."

Triumph in his eyes fell away as he looked at her more closely. Reaching out, he gently wiped a tear away. "Why are you crying?"

"I don't know. I guess because for a while I thought all of this was never going to happen. I've been wondering why you never mentioned where you wanted to build."

"I've been too afraid."

"Afraid of what?" This was news to her. From the time she'd first moved to his home, Henry had always acted confident and assured.

"You, if you wanna know the truth."

Anna was dumbstruck. "You're not making any sense."

Stepping to the side, he reached for her hands. When he held both securely within his own, he said, "Anna, you've given up so much. Sometimes, I know it's been particularly hard."

"It has, but I expected some things to be hard—they would have to be, don't you think? I mean, honestly, Henry, I was used to microwaving popcorn and zapping frozen dinners. But . . . but that doesn't mean my old ways were better. It's just taken some adjustment . . . and I have adjusted."

"I know you miss your music stations on the radio," he said, showing Anna that he'd truly listened to every story she'd told him about her past life. "I know you liked watching your soaps, too."

She fought a smile. "Believe me, I'm perfectly fine not watching *Days of Our Lives*."

"I'm just sayin' that I wouldn't have been shocked if you had changed your mind."

"Changed my mind—Henry, did you really think I could just up and leave you?" Anna didn't even try to contain her surprise. After everything they'd been through, she would have thought Henry was the last person in the world to doubt her love for him.

"I didn't think you would do something without thinking, but I could imagine that one day running your own home without any electricity might be terribly hard." He cleared his throat. "I've never taken your efforts for granted, Anna. You've given up a lot for me."

"I've gained more than I gave up," she said, knowing that words could never completely describe the peace she'd found with the Amish, the confidence that now surrounded her because she knew she was not alone—she was walking with the Lord. "I told my mother that yesterday when she came out to visit." Slowly, she added, "And, you know what? I think Mom is realizing that. No longer is she worried about me missing credit cards and cell phones. She's thinking about how happy I am, and how secure and comfortable I feel with you. How our love is the most important thing to me."

"I'm glad you two are talking more."

"Me too." Anna didn't know if she and her mother would ever completely put past arguments behind them, but she did think that they'd reached an agreement. She'd even stopped complaining about Henry's Amish life and how unsuitable he was for Anna. Sometime during the last year, she'd seemed to understand Anna and Henry were a good match. That it was their differences that complemented each other, and made each of their rough edges smoother.

Anna was truly grateful for her mother's change of heart. "Oh, Henry, I can hardly believe we'll be married at the beginning of May."

"May is not a long way off at all."

"No, though sometimes it still feels like a lifetime."

Reaching out for her, he murmured, "Sometimes, I think that, too."

His pronouncement made Anna very happy.

Sam had never minded getting dirty. That was a good thing, since at the moment, he was knee deep in mud and manure. He and Eli had been plowing and prepping the soil for the spring alfalfa crop over the last week, and while he didn't necessarily mind it, he had a very good feeling that he'd never get the earthy smell out of his clothes ever again.

Two rows over, Eli caught sight of his face and laughed heartily. "You look like you've been rolling in mud and came up the loser."

"I feel like it."

"In another day or two we'll be done and the soil will be better for our effort."

"That doesn't mean I won't be happy to be clean for a bit, though."

"You city types," Eli teased.

Eli chuckled again, then got back to work, carefully raking the soil with as much care as if he was handling baby chickens.

Sam did the same, though his mind kept drifting to other things, such as the people in the community. Most of the conversations he'd been part of had centered on the Lundy farm.

He liked Jonathan Lundy and was eager to help him repair his barn. Jonathan had a good job at the lumber factory and therefore could only work on Saturdays. A group of men—Sam included—had decided to help dismantle the building. Next would come a month of Saturdays in preparation to rebuild, culminating in a barn raising.

"Is Jonathan still thinking about raising his barn around the Brenneman wedding?"

"I believe so. May is a *gut* time to work. The weather will be warmer, and most of the planting will be done. Lots of men will be there to lend a helping hand." Straightening for a moment, Eli said, "It's a shame you won't be here for that."

"I'll try."

"Really? I thought you had to get back to the university."

"I do, but I want to do my part."

"You already have. No one will expect so much from you."

That bothered Sam more than he was willing to admit. Maybe because it was so true. No one here had ever accused him of not belonging, or for wanting to follow his dreams. Instead, they seemed to take his appearance in their lives the way they'd taken his leaving, with a shrug and a prayer that God had a plan for each of them.

Now that he thought of it, his English friends didn't treat him much differently. They were cordial and easy to work with. They respected his intelligence and his work ethic. But had they ever reached out to him in order to deepen their friendship?

More importantly, had he ever done that? As Sam felt his muscles expand and contract with the motion of his raking, he thought he never really had. No, more likely, he was constantly torn between two worlds, precariously balancing the views and values he was brought up with and the modern norms.

And there were quite a few modern conveniences he had enjoyed very much. Such as ESPN. He loved watching sports on television. He enjoyed baseball games and had become a fan of the Indians. He liked watching the college basketball games and rooting for the underdogs.

But was sports on TV all he needed?

"Let's clean up now, the sun's beginning to lay low."

"All right."

Sam walked his path, looking around with a sense of pleasure as he did so. His body felt worn, his mind free. He looked forward to a good meal and a solid night's sleep.

Those were the things that mattered. Not ambition and research papers.

# Chapter 9

"Oh, would you look at that?" Sam said to Winnie as they passed the Oberlins' farm. "Benjamin's got a new pup. Think he's going to be a good farm dog?"

Winnie turned just in time to see a speckled dog with popped up ears tagging alongside Ben and his plow. She chuckled. "He'll be good if he learns to mind the horses. Ben's got a team of four out today. That's a lot of hooves for one small *hund* to look out for."

"I betcha before long that dog is going to be taking a rest in the sun and leaving the hard work to his master."

"I imagine so." As the farm faded from view, she turned her attention once again to Sam. He'd been kind enough to offer to drive her to the doctor that morning. And though he said he didn't mind the errand, she still felt a bit guilty. The trip back and forth to the medical center was sure to take the better part of a day. "I hope Eli could spare you today."

"He can, I promise. We've been plowing and preparing the fields since I arrived. We are both happy to take a break."

That was yet another thing she liked about Sam. No matter what, he seemed to have a pleasant disposition. She'd rarely heard him ever complain. "I'm hoping to get some good news today."

"I hope you will. It looks like your skin is healing."

"I'll have some scars, but it's a small price to pay."

"That's the right attitude, Win. Good job," he added, sounding very much like the teacher he was.

The traffic got thick. She was still nervous enough around the large tractor trailers to fall silent so Sam could concentrate on the many vehicles around them. But every time there was silence, she found herself thinking about how their lives might have been if Sam had never left.

Moments later, he pulled into a parking place. As he unbuckled his seat belt, he grinned at her. "Now, don't you go running off without me, Winnie Lundy. Your brother would have my hat if I didn't insist you sit in your wheelchair."

Her cheeks heated at his gentle teasing. "Go on with you now, Samuel. I don't have all day."

But underneath her gruff words, she held these moments close to her heart.

A few days later, Winnie's ears were filled with jubilant shouts. "They're here! They're here!" Hannah shouted before racing Mary down the hall and jerking the door open with a flourish.

"Careful now, Hannah," Winnie called out, but her warning was ignored. Not hard to understand, since it was she who was stuck in the wheelchair, not her nieces.

Winnie sat quietly and listened to the three Miller men enter and get greeted with a round of excitement. It was hard to tell whose voice was whose as a chorus of "Hi, Sam! Hi, Eli! Hi, Caleb!" rang out.

As Katie joined them and conversation flowed, Winnie slumped as she continued to listen. Being in a wheelchair surely prevented her from being in the thick of things.

Slowly, she wheeled herself to the edge of the family room, so she could peek into the kitchen just enough to catch a bit of what was going on. Anything was better than seeing nothing.

After stomping their boots clean on the grate outside, the men finally came in. While Eli merely waved a hello and Caleb made a beeline toward the tray of vegetables and dip laying on the counter, Sam walked toward her. Winnie noticed that same amused look that always seemed to lurk behind his eyes. "How is your foot today?"

Looking at her cast, Winnie shrugged. "The same. I can't wait to get this cast off. I feel like I'm a prisoner. All I can do is watch from the sidelines." She winced then as she heard herself. "I'm sorry," she said quickly. "I sound like a petulant child. I know you didn't come over here just to hear me complain."

But instead of being taken aback by her clumsy words, he sat down on the tile in front of the bare fireplace. "I came over here for meatloaf and mashed potatoes, if you want the truth."

That admission brought her out of her pity party and made her laugh. "Samuel, you came to the right place. Katie is a right fine cook."

He pushed stray locks away from his forehead. "So, what have you been doing?"

"Quilting. Katie and I are making a wedding ring quilt for Henry and Anna. And, well, the girls are working on place mats for the couple."

"I figured you wouldn't be restless for long."

"I have been, but I'm trying not to let it get me down." She shrugged. "I like being busy."

"I like that about you."

"Well, you must like all Amish women, then. We all do a fine job of keepin' busy."

He chuckled. "Winnie, one thing's for sure. You are sure to never run out of things to say."

Once again, her penchant for speaking her mind made her feel self-conscious. Winnie swallowed and tried to pretend she wasn't moved by his attention. But, just as when they'd been in the truck together, she was. Still conscious of his gaze settling on her, she pushed the conversation along.

"So, what is new with you?"

"I got a new teaching assistant to help with labs. Her name is Kathleen and she's sharp as a whip."

"Kathleen?"

"Yep." Sam's eyes shone as he continued. "You would get a kick out of her, Winnie. She asked more questions than anyone I've ever met. And she carries around enough books for three people."

In spite of her jealousy, she was intrigued. "Why so many?"

"When I asked, she said they were more useful than her computer! She's going to keep me on my toes, I tell you that. Some days I feel like I can hardly keep up with her, she's so smart. Yesterday afternoon, she questioned the validity of one of the experiments we were working on. That led everyone into a rousing discussion. Two boys almost started yelling."

"It sounds exciting." But, really, his words brought forth a feeling of doom. In her world, she felt as confident and smart as anyone else. But in Sam's college world, she felt like a *dummkopp*—a dunce. When he started talking about scientific methods and organic compounds, she was completely lost.

Sam just kept talking, lost in his musings. "It was incredibly exciting. It's moments like that when I remember why I got into teaching. There's nothing like a group of interested, active minds."

"I'm sure they like you, too."

"They will, until I grill them over the reading and question all of their methods and theories. Then I have a feeling they won't like me very much." He chuckled. "Having to justify a hypothesis is a difficult task to perform."

Once she filtered out all the fancy language,

Winnie got to the heart of the matter. "Test-taking is part of learning, *jah*?"

Sam blinked, then smiled at her with dawning respect. "Of course, you're right. I forget just how sensible you are, Winnie. And forthright."

In spite of her best intentions to keep emotionally distant, Winnie was pleased. Rarely did people praise her for being sensible. In the past, most men she'd been interested in had preferred a more dreamy type of woman. They'd viewed her blunt way of seeing things as unfeminine. Of course, the only schooling she'd had was in the one-room Amish schoolhouse that he had been in, too. Like most other Amish, her formal schooling had ended at fourteen. After that, she'd focused on other important lessons, such as how to keep a good home.

"Sam, what are you doing?" Eli called out.

"Talking to Winnie."

"Well, come on over here, wouldja? Jonathan was just going to tell us about his plans for the new barn."

"You better go, the plans are exciting, to be sure," she said quickly when he hesitated.

"Okay." Standing up, he grasped the handles of her chair. "I'll push you into the kitchen. That way you won't have to be here by yourself."

"It's okay. I can move myself, and well, I've heard plenty about the barn plans. Go on."

As soon as he was out of sight, Winnie rested her

head against the padded fabric of the wheelchair. Oh, but he made her heart race, he was so terribly good-looking. She liked the way he was interested and seemed to care about so many things. There always seemed to be a hint of mischief lying beneath his eyes, like he was thinking of so much more than he ever spoke aloud.

No, there was nothing plodding and quiet about Sam.

Once, at the hospital, she'd noticed a pair of women looking at him with interest. One had whispered to the other. After a moment, they'd both giggled. Winnie could only imagine the interest he inspired among the women at his college.

That new Kathleen was probably smitten with Samuel, too. Valiantly, Winnie decided that was good. After all, he would be a fine husband for some woman.

The door opened again. Moments later, the welcome voices of Anna and Henry joined the throng. To her pleasure, both Katie and Anna soon left the kitchen and joined her.

"We couldn't take that conversation a moment longer," Katie said as soon as she sat down. "Plans and more plans. Those men are excited about every nail!"

"Henry's acting as if it is *his* dream barn they're fixin' to construct! These men are planning for it to be double the size and twice as sturdy."

"It's too bad Sam and Eli's parents aren't here," Winnie said. "They'd help settle everyone down. Mr. Miller always has been the voice of reason."

"I don't think even Mr. Miller could settle this talk down," Katie murmured. "Eli can't seem to stop talkin' about a bigger tack room, a work shed, and even a storage area for the house." She paused. "'Course, a storage area might come in handy. There's never enough space in the kitchen."

"Don't get roped in," Winnie advised. "If you give those men any encouragement, they'll never stop the plans."

"Like they would even think about listening to us."

Anna rolled her eyes. "What do we know anyway?"

Katie puffed up her chest. "Nothing about barn building, only about keeping a home."

"And we all know that is nothing like organizing a fine barn."

Unable to stop herself, Winnie erupted into giggles, and her friends joined in. "Soon enough, the men will be having to help us with wedding plans. I'm so glad you aren't going to delay the wedding, Anna."

"I am, too, though I've been concerned about doing the right thing." With a worried look at Katie, Anna murmured, "Are you sure you don't mind a celebration in the middle of so much chaos? I feel awfully selfish."

"No one would accuse you of being selfish, Anna," Katie said. "You've put a lot of your own needs to the side time and again. It's time to put yourself first."

Anna's gaze softened before murmuring, "Henry's worried about the timing of the wedding, too."

"He shouldn't worry, and neither should you," Winnie said. "Whether you get married or not, it won't change what already happened. Now we'll get to have something to look forward to."

"And we need a celebration soon," Katie said. "Too much doom and gloom will only keep us up at night."

Anna looked at Katie. "Your mother said the same thing."

Katie chuckled. "More and more, I fear I am sounding like my mother. Who would have ever thought!"

Anna turned to Katie. "How is Jonathan holding up?"

Katie paused. "I think the mystery of who started the fire is bothering Jonathan more than he lets on. His heart and mind want him to forgive and forget, but how can he if no one claims responsibility?"

"Maybe we can help?" Anna ventured.

"How?" Winnie asked. "I don't know who we would even talk to."

Katie nibbled her bottom lip for a moment, then

spoke. "Winnie, remember how we used to go to the Weavers' home for singings?"

"*Jah*. They were a wonderful couple." Looking at Anna, Winnie explained. "Often a family will host singings for the community's teenagers on Sunday evenings. It's a time for young people to get a chance to be together and have fun."

Anna scowled. "And what do singings have to do with us?"

"I think we ought to host a few singings and visit with the kids a bit. We might learn something," Katie said practically.

Winnie's eyes danced. "It will be like we are playing detective."

"That could be dangerous," Anna warned. "Whoever set the barn on fire has got to be feeling guilty. Plus, what will we do if we do find out who did it? Tell the authorities?"

Katie sighed. "I haven't thought that far ahead. All I know is that it's hard to forgive someone who hasn't sought forgiveness. And I think Jonathan needs that." Katie shrugged. "Besides, he doesn't have time to ask questions of people. He's working at the lumberyard, and at tearing down the barn."

"Henry is busy, too. We've had a lot of guests at the inn."

"Eli's got planting and Caleb to watch," Winnie added. "And Sam . . ." Winnie stopped, feeling self-conscious, especially when Katie looked at her curiously.

"Yes?"

"Nothing. I was just going to say that I'm sure Sam has a lot to do, too."

"Of course he does. He's busy with things at his college. And his own life—right?" Anna said the last as a question.

"Yes. Well, I mean, I suppose." But wouldn't it be wonderful if he wanted to stay with them? Wouldn't it be something if his life was right there in their community, too?

"Sam is a good man," Katie said slowly, but with a tone edged in steel. "I'm glad he's been so helpful. But he's not really one of us any longer. We can't expect him to drop everything and help us build a barn."

No matter what happened in the future, Winnie knew Sam had become a part of her world. Again. "He may not live here with us, but I know he still cares. It's not like he is shunned."

"That is true," Katie agreed slowly. Without even trying to be subtle, she glanced over her shoulder toward the kitchen door. "And he did stop by today. That is new."

After glancing at the door as well, Anna turned to Winnie, her eyes narrowing with speculation. "He sure is a handsome man, isn't he?"

"I only have eyes for Jonathan, but I do have to admit that I've always liked his sunny personality," Katie said.

"He's been a good brother to Eli and friend to

Jonathan, visiting me like he did in the hospital."

With a mischievous smile, Anna said, "Are you sure he only visited you for his brother?"

"Of course."

"Oh."

And Winnie felt bad. After all, she knew exactly what she was doing—shutting out her friend. But it couldn't be helped. She couldn't entertain the feelings in her heart.

There wasn't anything anyone could do.

Winnie had finally fallen hard, and now that she realized that there was nothing she could do in order to make things better, she was going to have to resign herself to a life alone.

Perhaps she would soon find greater value in her work, or in simply being an aunt instead of a mother.

But she didn't think so.

# Chapter 10

Everything was going too fast. The rumors and talk were snowballing into a big heap of trouble that couldn't be escaped.

And David had surely tried.

But there was no avoiding the talk and gossip. Everywhere he looked, people were speculating about the cause of the fire and how the Lundys weren't about to give up. Jonathan's struggle to forgive whoever had started the fire was a cause of much discussion.

Men and boys alike were finding it hard not to take sides. Some thought Jonathan was right to have dug in his heels like he had. After all, someone had to take responsibility for the fire, it was the right thing to do. Others thought Jonathan had lost sight of the Bible's teachings and of the *Ordnung* as well. Compassion and forgiveness were qualities to be proud of, not something to be ignored when the timing wasn't right.

It had been hard to stay out of all the discussions, but he had done his best.

And still, David's hands wouldn't heal. Sores had formed on his burns, stinging and scabbing. They made the most menial tasks an effort and filled with pain. Almost every night, he'd taken to soaking his hands in warm water, hoping and praying for the skin to mend. But it was as if the

Lord wasn't listening to him . . . or perhaps He was making him pay for his lies and secrets.

"David, you done cleaning the stalls yet?"

No matter how hard he tried otherwise, David always found himself flinching the moment he heard his *daed*'s rough voice. "Yes."

"Come over, then."

After putting aside the rake and removing the soiled hay from the premises, he rushed to meet his father, who was looking at him impatiently.

"I don't know what is taking you so long these days. And let me see those hands of yours."

Dutifully, David held out his palms, concentrating on keeping his face expressionless as he flattened them out. But oh, how they ached and burned.

To his surprise, his father looked concerned. "They are in a bad way. How come they are so ripped up? What did you do?"

"I don't know."

"Sure you do. No one hurts hands like that and doesn't know what happened. What did you do? The truth, now."

The truth. Oh, how his father loved asking for honesty.

But everyone in the family knew from experience that the only truthfulness Amos wanted to hear were words that didn't upset him.

But . . . David also knew the Lord wanted him to speak of the truth, too. Maybe if he finally admitted what happened, his hands would start to heal, and the sleepless nights that plagued him would be a thing of the past.

"David?"

"I . . . Well, you see . . ."

"Stop your sputtering. Speak like a man."

Here was his chance. If he'd been braver or smarter or more confident, David knew he would have seized the moment and told all. But he was afraid of his father. He didn't trust him. Too many times, he'd met with a sharp comment or quick hand for speaking without thinking.

Now David made sure he never did that. Quickly he made up a story. "I was mending one of the back fences and cut my palms on the barbed wire. It's nothing."

Reaching out, his *daed* gripped his hand and looked at it more closely. David's pulse raced. Was it obvious that the sores were from burns not cuts?

"Did your mother look at them?"

"No. There was no need. I'm fine."

After eyeing his face another long moment, his father pointed to a basket laden with baked goods. "I want you to take that basket to the Lundys' for your mother."

"What?"

The burst of surprise earned him a sharp look. "I said, take that basket to the Lundys', and be quick about it. Your mother has been in a charitable mind. She's been baking for Jonathan and his family morning, noon, and night. Go take it over now."

Slipping on his straw hat, David nodded, then hurried to comply. He'd just picked up the basket and started toward Palmer, their sorrel, when his father's voice cracked through the quiet. "And David?"

*"Jah?"* He didn't turn around.

"Don't be so foolish with the fencing again. I'm to be needin' every available hand to help with the planting. You should know better."

"I learned from my mistake," David murmured. "It won't happen again."

David couldn't believe he was at the Lundys' again. In the broad daylight, the burnt cinders of the barn made him feel terribly ill and queasy.

"David Hostetler?" little Mary Lundy called out from the front porch. "Is that you?"

"Where's Katie? I mean, your *mamm*?" David still sometimes had to remind himself that Katie Brenneman was Mrs. Lundy now.

"She's inside. Go on in."

David stared at the shut door. To him, that door seemed to symbolize everything that he'd been trying to do—put up as many obstacles as possible so he wouldn't have to face the consequences.

Mary scampered off her chair and with a swift turn of the wrist, flew open the door and raced inside. After a second, she peeked out again. "You comin' ain'tcha?"

*"Jah."* Once in the kitchen, the heavenly aroma of baked ham and stewed apples floated over him. "Mrs. Lundy, I've a basket for you from my *mamm.*"

"She's such a dear." Katie slipped the basket on the counter, then linked a hand around his elbow. "I just baked a ham. How about a snack?"

Though the ham did smell enticing, he couldn't leave fast enough. Pushing his hat back, David shook his head. "No. *Danke,* I've gotta get back."

Her eyes widened at the sight of his hand. "Whatever happened to you?" She reached out and snatched a hand before he could even think. "Oh, my! You have an infection!"

"I'm fine."

"I think not. Come here by the sink and we'll try to doctor you up a bit."

"I don't want—"

"She likes doing things her way," Mary chirped up. "You'd best just let her do it."

"Mary's right," Katie said as she pulled out a hand and guided him closer. "Now, come here, and let me see if I can help."

David thought his heart would stop beating when Katie clasped his right palm, clucked over the swollen areas, opened a jar of ointment, then gently rubbed some over each wound. "How did you get so hurt?"

He claimed the same lie. "Barbed wire."

"This is *gut* medicine for burns, but I think it will help cuts, too."

Before he could say another word, she pulled out a clean strip of linen and hastily wrapped his hand. "Keep them wrapped up, David. It will hold off the infection."

"Yes."

After doing the same with his other hand, she spooned another bit of ointment into a leftover jelly jar. "Put this on morning and night and your cuts will be better in no time."

Backing toward the door, he said, "I've gotta go." Turning, he fled the confinement of the Lundys' kitchen as quick as his feet would take him.

And had the bandages off well before he unsaddled Palmer.


Sam made the drive from Eli's home to his college campus in under an hour, which felt like a minor miracle. Sometimes the traffic on I–71 got so congested it reminded him of a colony of ants, with everyone simply marching along.

After parking in his assigned spot, he nodded to a few students he recognized around the central fountain, by-passed the library commons area, and hightailed it into the agricultural building.

However, there was nothing otherworldly about the commotion that greeted him once he walked to his department's offices.

"Hi, Professor Miller!" Zach, one of his students who worked in the office, called out. "I'm taking a message, but I'll be off the phone in just one sec."

"No problem." Standing in front of Zach's desk, Sam found that he needed a moment to adjust to the noise and commotion. Phones rang, music blared, and everywhere he looked students were standing in twos and threes and talking as loud as possible.

Once, he used to find the activity and noise energizing. Now, especially after spending the morning with his Amish friends and family, all the noise and lights seemed annoying. Almost unnecessary and distracting from what was really important to him.

With a click, Zach set down the phone. "Sorry"—before Sam could say a word, the student rushed on—"Professor Miller, this place has been going crazy. And you've gotten so many messages and papers, there's hardly an empty inch on your desk."

"I was only gone a week. I couldn't have that many messages, surely."

"You do. Once more, everything's been slowly falling apart." Lifting up a stack of slim yellow papers, Zach frowned. "First off, you've got about twenty-five messages to return, not to mention all the notes here from students wanting to speak with you."

"Any reason why?"

"They want to know if you've graded their latest quizzes."

"I haven't."

"Don't tell them that, they're nervous wrecks," Zach said, clicking open a screen on his computer.

"I'll tell the kids they're going to have to wait a few more days. I've had some family commitments."

That stopped Zach's fingers. "I've never heard you mention your family before."

"Well, I have one," he replied wryly.

"I'm sorry how I sounded. It's just that I've never heard you speak of your family. Do they live nearby?"

"About an hour east."

"Is everything okay?"

"Yes, they um, just needed a hand. A sister of a friend was in the hospital and they needed a translator. And someone to look after her."

"A translator?"

"Yes. My family is Amish."

"Amish? Like the old-fashioned people?"

Thinking of how well Eli was juggling spring planting, helping with the Lundy barn, and looking after Caleb by himself, Sam chuckled. "You'd be surprised at how forward thinking they can be."

"You know what I mean. I mean, don't they wear hats and white caps and long skirts and ride around in buggies and stuff?"

"Yes." It made Sam uncomfortable to hear his

whole family's way of life reduced to funny clothes and transportation methods. But, well, that's part of why he'd always been reluctant to tell people he'd grown up Amish, wasn't it?

Zach turned completely his way, work forgotten. "So, a translator, huh? What do you guys speak?"

"We speak English."

He waved a hand. "Come on, Professor. You know what I mean. Don't they or you speak another language, too? Dutch?"

Well, obviously he was going to have to talk about this, even if he didn't want to. "The Amish speak Pennsylvania Dutch, but it's a derivative of German, not Dutch. But everyone learns to speak and write in English as well." Before Zach could ask any more questions, Sam said, "I'll go get busy. Sounds like we don't want to get any further behind."

"No, we don't." Zach looked at him curiously, then shook his head. "So, what do you want me to tell the people who call this afternoon? Are you scheduling visits and taking appointments, or would you rather Kathleen handled the bulk of them?"

"I'll see students. Kathleen's bound to be ready for a break." Approaching the students milling around outside his office door, he said, "Sorry, guys, I don't have the quizzes graded yet."

"Can't you just tell us how we did?" one asked.

"I mean it—I really haven't had a moment to

grade anything. I had some family commitments to take care of."

The same blank stares met him that Zach had used just a few moments ago. "You all go on, now. I'll post the grades as soon as I can."

With a few grumbles, the students turned and walked away. "I didn't know Professor Miller had a family," one whispered.

And that was the problem, Sam realized. Over the last few years, he'd been so intent on his work, he'd done little else. Now he was paying for it.

Suddenly feeling overwhelmed, he unlocked his office door and turned on the light. "I'll be in all afternoon and tomorrow," he turned and said to Zach.

"I'll pass that on." Finally looking mollified, Zach added, "Do you need anything, Professor?"

"Sure. Order in a couple of sandwiches and soda when you get time, okay?"

"Italian club?"

"Sure," he replied as he wandered into the sanctity of his office.

But it didn't feel homey at all. Instead, it felt like it often did on Fridays, when he was anxious for the weekend to begin. The room felt small and confining. Dark and claustrophobic. Utilitarian and serviceable. Its lack of window made him feel like he was working in a glorified janitor's closet.

What was even more vexing was the idea that he'd been happy here for quite a while.

Correction—he'd been trying to make himself happy here. But perhaps that had been like trying to fit a square peg in a round hole.

He'd just sat down when the phone rang. Instead of waiting for Zach to screen the call, he picked it up himself. "Miller."

"Professor, I'm worried about my internship," Andrew Thrust said in a rush. "No one's contacted me yet."

"I'll look into it. As far as I know, they haven't made any decisions yet. I'll call you next week."

"But what if they don't accept me? I need this in the worst way."

"I know. Hang in there, Andrew. What's meant to be will happen."

"Oh. Um, well thanks, Professor. You're the best."

He'd just hung up when the phone rang again. Now he was feeling a little bit sorry for Zach. No wonder the guy was looking so ragged. "Miller."

But instead of another question or demand, it was the sweetest voice ever on the other end of the line. "Samuel?"

"Winnie. Hi." He didn't even try to hide the concern he was feeling. "Is everything okay?"

"Oh. Yes. I had just heard you left this morning. I um, wondered if you made it back all right. I hope you don't mind my calling on the telephone."

"No. I don't mind at all." Actually, her concern made him smile for the first time all day. It had been a long time since anyone had worried about him and let him know it so transparently. It had been even longer since he'd felt so pleased that someone cared. "I just walked into my office a few minutes ago. The drive was not a problem at all. Where are you? I know you can't be calling from home."

"I'm actually at the Brennemans'. Mrs. Brenneman was kind enough to let me help out at the inn today. I'm helping with some mending and ironing. It's one of the few things I can do while sitting down."

"I'm glad you're not alone." He'd been coming to realize that Winnie was so self-sufficient, it was unlikely that she'd ever make an issue of being bored or lonely. But she still would feel those things.

"I'm glad, too. I'd like to feel helpful and not a burden for a change." After a long pause, she chuckled. "I'm sorry, it just occurred to me that you must be terribly busy, and here I am, chattering on about nothing. I'll let you go."

He hadn't thought she was chattering at all. And, in fact, he found the pleasant way she had about speaking calmed his nerves and lifted his spirits. It put everything in perspective. Just hearing her positive approach to responsibilities made him rethink the dozen things on his to-do list. Perhaps now he wouldn't look at them as simply burdens, but opportunities. "I'm glad you called. Perhaps when

I come back to help Jonathan with the barn we'll see each other again."

"Oh, yes. When will that be?"

"In a week or two, I'm thinking. But if Eli needs more help in the fields, I might come back sooner."

"I'm glad. Oh! I mean, it will be nice for Eli to have that help, you know."

How long had it been since he was around a woman who didn't even try to hide her feelings? "I think it will be nice, too."

"Well . . . I best get going."

"Thanks for calling, Winnie. I'll visit you when I go see Eli."

"Yes. Well, *dats gut*."

After he hung up, Sam found himself staring at the phone, and wishing that he was sitting across from Winnie instead of just being surprised to hear her voice.

Her words were so full of expression. She had no need to hide her emotions. It made everyone else seem too guarded.

He hoped she really was healing as well as she said she was.

"Professor Miller," Zach called out, bringing back reality. "Aaron Knight is on the phone. Can you meet with him now?"

"Sure. Tell him to come on over." He might as well do his best to adopt Winnie's attitude and be thankful for his work. After all, it would keep him busy until he could see her again.

# Chapter 11

"Were we just as boisterous and noisy during our singings?" Winnie whispered to Katie as they watched the crowd of teens congregate in the front of the Brenneman's Bed and Breakfast. "I don't remember being so rowdy, but maybe we were."

Katie grinned. "Oh, we were."

As one boy told a joke and the rest of the assemblage roared in laughter, Winnie frowned. "Truly? I seem to recall being more circumspect."

"You weren't." Loud laughter mixed with taunts and jokes as the kids went about building a bonfire that Henry was loosely supervising. Katie leaned closer to be heard. "However, I will admit that they seem to be gettin' louder with every passing minute."

"Do they seem too loud?" Anna asked as she walked over to join them. Eyes dancing, she said, "They don't seem bad, just like they're having fun." As one girl visibly flirted with a brown-haired boy, Anna chuckled. "It all looks pretty tame. When I think of the things I was doing at sixteen and seventeen, I feel like cringing. I wasn't at friends' houses either."

"Where did you spend your free time?" Winnie asked. Though Anna didn't speak about her English life too often, Winnie enjoyed hearing stories about the things she did.

"Anywhere there weren't watching eyes. Friends' cars. Movie theaters, parks." Her eyes lit up. "Shopping malls. Oh, I loved to go shopping."

"These kids are doing that, too, sometimes you know. Remember, most have started their *rumspringa*," Katie said.

"I betcha kids are the same, no matter where they are," Winnie mused. "I went to plenty of these singings and all I seem to remember is feeling the need to yell and laugh and be as loud as possible. Ach, what a time we had. I'd forgotten how special it was."

Anna frowned. "Now, here's something I've been wanting to ask, but haven't had the nerve. If it's called a singing, how come I don't hear any music?"

"Oh, Anna. Sometimes people sing, but mostly singings are just an excuse to have a good time with everyone. In the fall, there are bonfires and hay rides. Winter brings sledding and ice skating in the moonlight. Spring and summer, long walks and picnics."

Anna shook her head. "It sounds like fun. It's too bad more English teens aren't as satisfied with such wholesome pursuits."

"Don't let the clothes fool you," Winnie warned. "These teens are feeling the same things any other teens in America are . . . restless."

Katie crossed her arms over her chest. "Which brings us to our reason for being here. Who do you think is our likely smoker?"

Winnie scanned the crowd, but to her eye, no one looked any different than they usually did. "No telling by standing here. I suppose it's time we all went out and mingled. We'll only learn by asking questions."

Anna raised a brow. "And hope someone mentions setting fire to your barn?"

"Try not to be that obvious," Katie said before stepping down the stairs and joining a group. Within seconds, she was chatting up a storm with all the teenagers, looking for a moment no older than the teens surrounding her.

"Boy, she's good," Winnie said.

"That's Katie. On the outside, she looks to be the easiest person in the world to know. So sweet and merry, too. I always pity the person who assumes there's not much more to Katie than pretty cheeks and beautiful blue eyes."

Winnie chuckled. "I may not have her eyes, but I've got crutches and an injury to play up. And you, Anna, have the best thing of all to discuss."

"What's that?"

"The most perfect topic in the world for a crowd of teenagers who ache to be in love—a wedding!"

Anna beamed. "That's right! I do."

They mixed in with the kids. Sure enough, the girls did enjoy speaking with Anna about wedding plans.

Before they knew it, though, everyone was also interested in her past life. A few kids asked questions about high school and college, about malls and movies and things of the outside world.

Anna answered readily, and then to Winnie's amazement, she started talking about how she'd tried smoking when she was a teen.

Winnie kept a sharp eye on everyone's reactions. But no one seemed either particularly interested or surprised by Anna's revelations. The girls just shrugged and asked instead about rumors they'd heard of people piercing their belly buttons.

But then, just as they were about to give up their pitiful efforts of detective work, Winnie noticed one boy looking at Caleb Miller in alarm. It took a moment to place his name. He was quiet, somewhat shorter than most others, and usually stayed in the background during gatherings. But his strawberry blond hair triggered a memory and she knew at once who he was—David Hostetler.

All Winnie knew about the family was that there were a great many *kinner*—eight or nine, and that Mr. Hostetler was terribly determined to embrace only old ways. He'd always seemed strict, too. Winnie had rarely seen him laugh or make jokes like her father often did.

Just as she decided to walk over to see why David looked so ill at ease, two boys asked for more lemonade. Moments later, David was gone.

David walked as quickly as he'd been able to the back field. As soon as he'd felt safe, he crouched down and tried to catch his breath, but it was hard, he was shaking so badly. Katie Lundy knew. *She knew*.

Otherwise, there's no way she'd have asked the questions she did.

"David, are you okay?" Caleb Miller asked. "You raced out of the gathering so quick—like, I thought you were gonna get sick or something."

"I'm fine. I just had to be by myself for a second."

When Caleb's eyes widened and he backed up a step, David fumbled over his words again. "I mean, I didn't know anyone had seen me leave. But you can stay, if you want."

Around them, the earth smelled fresh and new. Freshly plowed. Alive and rich. Much of the dark rows looked the same as their farm. And because he knew just how hard it was to keep things looking good, David walked toward the edge of the land. Once safely on the side, they both sat down.

"So, what's wrong? You look like you saw a ghost."

"Nothin's wrong. I just didn't like how Katie was staring at me."

A line formed between Caleb's brows. "Like how?"

"Like she knew something bad about me."

"What would she know? And who cares anyway? All we're doing is bein' kids."

"No, this was different. I think she was staring at

me because she thought I did something wrong." With a sinking feeling, he was sure everything in his life was about to fall apart. "She's going to go make up something to my father and I'm going to get punished."

"You need to stop worrying and get out more." Caleb laughed. "Why were you staring at her anyway? I thought you liked Krista."

"Krista wasna paying attention to me. She's all eyes for the older boys all of a sudden."

"Well, if Katie was looking our way, I bet it was because she remembered how I used to follow her around like a puppy. That's my secret," Caleb said, tucking his chin to his chest for a moment. "I used to fancy myself in love with her."

"She's old."

"*Jah,* but she's pretty."

"She's a lot older."

Caleb shrugged. "Not that much. Anyway, I never thought anything would happen between me and her—I'm just saying that I used to have a little crush on her."

Taking a chance, David murmured, "I think she knows I've been smoking."

Caleb's eyes widened. "Truly? Why do you think that?"

"I saw . . . I saw her looking at me while Anna was talking about all that."

"About what?"

He could hardly say the words. "About when,

you know . . . the barn burnt down. The fire officials said it was from someone smoking. When she looked at me, it was like Katie Lundy knew I'd been doing something I wasn't supposed to." He swallowed hard, wanting to also tell Caleb about how she'd doctored his hands, but didn't dare. If Caleb knew the truth about him, he'd tell on him, for sure.

"Well, we know you weren't the one who started the fire, so what does it matter?"

"I'm afraid she's going to say something to her husband or to my parents."

"That's not too bad, is it?" Caleb shrugged. "Who cares if she did think you were smoking anyway? I know even my brother Eli tried it once or twice, and he's practically perfect. I don't know about Samuel, but I betcha he's done all kinds of things out there among the English."

"You don't know what would happen if my father found out. He'd be really mad."

"Hey? Why are you so worried? You stopped smoking anyhow. I heard you tellin' the guys how you didn't care about smoke rings no more." He paused, looking at him more closely. "At least, I thought you stopped. Didn't you?"

"Sure I stopped." Suddenly, he knew he had to ask for a favor. "Caleb, I stopped, but I still got the cigarettes and stuff. I don't have a safe place to throw them out. Would you mind if I gave them to you?"

Caleb lifted a hand in protest. "I don't want all that. What am I gonna do with them?"

"My *daed* hardly lets me go anywhere. And there're eight kids in my house. I'm never alone. Not like you." Thinking quickly, he said, "I was hopin' that maybe if I gave you my lighter and pack of cigarettes you could get rid of them for me."

Caleb bit his lip. "I don't know . . ."

"I wouldn't ask you if there was anyone else." Oh, he was so ashamed. "But there isn't. Would you take them from me? I could drop them over at your house tonight."

"Tonight?"

"Yeah. Sometimes I sneak out."

"Then you get rid of it."

"You can't just toss those things in a field or something. They've got to be gotten rid of somewhere away from here. Like McClusky's store."

"I don't know."

"It's been weeks since I had any free time to go to McClusky's. I've got no one else to ask, Caleb. Please say you'll do this."

A strange look fell over Caleb's face. "Sure," he mumbled in a rush, his eyes now darting around like he was nervous to be seen with David. Uncomfortable. "Go ahead and give them to me."

"When? Later on tonight?" Thinking quickly, he said, "We can leave now and I'll give you the lighter."

"No. By the time the singing's over, my brothers will be looking for me."

David was so eager to get those things out of his life, he pushed a little more. "Tomorrow night?"

"Ah. Yeah, sure." Caleb stepped away. "I'm gonna go now." A new look shone in his eyes. Worry and trepidation. Fear.

"I guess I'm just acting crazy." David tried to smile, but he knew it came out sickly. He'd pushed too hard and now Caleb distrusted him. "I'll walk back to the party."

Caleb's eyes cleared. "Okay." Bumping his shoulder in a friendly way, Caleb added, "When we get back, I dare ya to go over and talk to Krista and her friends."

"She won't want to talk to me."

"Sure she will. If you hadn't been so worried about Katie Lundy looking at you, you would've seen her interest. Come on, why don'tcha? The singing's almost over. If we wait much longer, we'll have to wait a whole 'nother week to make plans."

"You go first."

"All right. My *daed* said I could start using the courting buggy. I mean to use it for courting, too."

Their pace quickened as they walked toward the others.

But though his pace was strong and purposeful, David still couldn't stop shaking. He hadn't liked how Katie Lundy had looked at him, and worse, he was scared to death of facing the reality of what he almost did. He'd almost admitted to Caleb that he'd been in her barn.

Caleb nudged him. "Come on, don't keep standing over here by the tree, looking like you're trying to hold it up. There're too many pretty girls over here to talk to. Let's go see if they want to go walking with us."

"I'll be there in a minute."

Suddenly Caleb looked worried. "Some are looking at us. Come on, David, I don't wanna go over there by myself."

"I mean it, go ahead."

"I hope you figure things out soon," he said over his shoulder in obvious disgust. "I'm going. If Krista goes out walkin' with me, don't be mad."

"I won't."

Caleb didn't wait another moment. Sure enough, he sauntered over to the girls, all full of smiles. Before long, one of them was walking by his side, gazing at him in happiness.

Caleb had it so easy. He was good-looking and strong, and a whole year older. His family laughed, and he even had a brother who was smart, so smart he became a professor or something.

David Hostetler was none of those things. His body didn't seem to want to grow. He was flustered around girls.

He hated his life at home.

All he had was the ability to make smoke rings.

And now he couldn't ever tell another person about it.


"You're looking mighty dreamy-eyed, Anna," Irene Brenneman said when she found her on the porch two evenings later.

Anna started. "I'm sorry. My mind went wandering."

"Thinking about the wedding?"

"Yes. And the fact that my parents will be coming to visit for two days."

To her surprise, Irene joined her on the top step, moving the bowl of sugar snap peas Anna was shelling. "I'm looking forward to getting to know your parents better, Anna. Each time they've visited, I've come to see a lot of them in you."

Anna liked how Irene had phrased that. She liked imagining that she'd inherited good qualities from her parents, despite the fact she'd chosen a lifestyle drastically different from theirs. "They are nice people. Good people."

"And you are a wonderful girl."

Irene's compliment warmed her heart. Henry was a fine man, and Anna imagined Irene and John had harbored their share of doubts about Anna's suitability for him. "They might be a little demanding. They aren't used to this lifestyle."

"Then they came to the right place, hmm? We

are, of course, a bed and breakfast. We cater to all sorts of English. Don't worry so. John and I will make them welcome."

Anna slowly turned to Irene. "Are you sure you're okay with me marrying your son? After all, my past—"

"*Jah*. I am sure."

"But perhaps you should know—"

Irene cut her off again. "I don't need to know more than I do now, Anna. We all have checkered pasts. Even me."

"Even you?"

With a hint of humor, Irene's eyes sparkled. "Well, some pasts might be a bit more checkered than others, but what's important is what is between you and the Lord. It all comes back to the Lord, Anna."

Pulling the bowl closer, Anna murmured, "I'll get these beans done for supper."

With a sigh, Irene pulled herself up to her feet. "I suppose I must get to work, too. I've hired two girls to come help me clean today. Watch out for them, will ya? I don't want to see them yakking away in the guest rooms when there's woodwork to be oiled."

"I'll keep a close eye on them, for sure." Digging her hands into the cool nest of beans, Anna grabbed another pod and broke it cleanly.

And as she thought about Irene's words, and how God was looking out for all of them, even in the darkest of days, she reflected how much better she felt. How much more at peace she was living the Amish ways. It was like she was made for this lifestyle all along. And all the hardships she had gone through in the past were directing her to this place, and the man that she loved.

Closing her eyes, Anna said a prayer of thanks. Yes, things were so much easier when she remembered she wasn't alone. And never had been.

# Chapter 12

Now that she wasn't in so much pain, Winnie was settling into her old routines. Though she was anxious to go back to work at the store, she didn't mind helping Katie with the girls and the housework as often as she could.

Now, as they were working on Anna's wedding ring quilt, Katie seemed particularly thoughtful. Winnie had quite a few thoughts of her own— mainly about Samuel Miller, so she didn't mind the quiet in the least.

But Katie broke the peaceful moment before Winnie had even needed to thread her needle more than once. "You know, I can't help but think about the fire. No matter what I do, my mind keeps drifting back to that."

"I don't know if hosting the singing helped much. Do you?"

Biting her lip, Katie shrugged. "Only time will tell."

Winnie leaned over the fabric and concentrated on making straight, even stiches. Recalling how most of the teenagers hadn't been especially eager to speak with them, she said, "Goodness, Katie, I don't know why we thought the teens would tell us anything."

"They were friendly."

"That is true. But it's not like they were eager to go about telling us any deep, dark secrets." With a touch of sentiment, Winnie imagined things weren't so much different now than when she was their age. Teens were rarely in a hurry to seek out the advice of someone older.

"I guess not. But I might understand their problems more than they think."

Winnie nodded. She knew of Holly, the English girl Katie'd befriended during her running around time. Though Katie hadn't spoken of it much, Winnie knew Katie had once fancied an English boy, Holly's brother.

"There wasn't anyone who you thought acted suspiciously?" Winnie asked.

"The only one was David, who I know hangs around Caleb quite a bit. Do you know him?"

"Only the family. They keep to themselves."

"That David's a strange one. Kind of timid and nervous." Chuckling, Katie shook her head. "Forget I even mentioned him. He's too nervous to do anything without his parents' permission. Gosh, when I was talking to him about our plans for the barn raising, he looked scared to death. I don't think he's very handy with tools either. He hurt his hands on some barbed wire something awful."

"I guess we'll just have to keep thinking, then," Winnie said as they drifted back toward working in silence.

After all that worrying about how to discover the fire starter's identity, Winnie came across a clue a few days later—when she least expected it. It was there in the buggy next to hers—mixed in with a canvas bag of groceries and a basket of dry pinto beans. A carelessly tossed package of cigarettes.

She looked around. Whose buggy was this? As she used her crutches to peer a little closer into the buggy, she heard footsteps crossing from Sam McClusky's general store to the parking lot.

"Winnie? Miss Lundy? Is something wrong?"

She started. Turning away from the evidence, she met the golden-hued eyes of Caleb Miller. Oh, dear. Had Katie been right? Could Caleb really have been the person who'd started the fire?

What should she do now? Tell Eli?

But what if Eli didn't even know Caleb was smoking? Surely it wasn't her place to tell him! Yet . . . he and Sam had done so much for her brother and Katie. Wasn't it her duty to let them know what she'd seen?

More distressing, what if they did know something but were choosing to keep it secret?

"Winnie? You look kind of funny. Do you need to sit down or somethin'?"

"No, Caleb. I'm fine," she lied. "Sorry my mind drifted. I, uh, just saw something that reminded me of my past."

He cocked his head to one side. "Really? What did you see?"

She couldn't blame Caleb for his surprise, she was having trouble at the moment thinking of a single memory that would have anything to do with his buggy. But still, it was time to come up with an excuse!

"Yes, I, uh, saw your basket of dried beans and was remembering a time I cooked them for Jonathan and the girls. They were truly verra bad. Jonathan was sick for a whole night, I tell you that." There. Now he would look into his basket and realize what she'd seen. He'd be flustered and tell her why he'd been smoking. And, more importantly, what happened the night the barn burned.

But instead of looking guilty, he just smiled. "That must have been a terribly long time ago."

"Not so long."

When she made a point to stare at the basket again, Caleb glanced at it, too. For a moment his grin faltered as it was obvious they were both staring at the exposed carton of cigarettes.

Furtively, he reached a hand in through the open back window and not-so-stealthily tried to cover them up. Winnie kept her expression wide-eyed and innocent. It would be better for Caleb to offer an explanation instead of her pressing him for one.

But still, she didn't look away when he met her gaze sheepishly. "I guess I shouldn't even try to hide them, should I? You going to tell my brothers?"

"About the beans? Or . . . about what else was in that basket?"

"You know. The cigarettes."

"You shouldn't be smoking, you know." Oh, she half expected lightning to burst out of the clouds above her, she sounded so very prim. Still, she waited. Waited for him to admit that he'd been in the barn.

Waited for him to tell her he'd made an awful mistake.

"I know." He shrugged. "They aren't mine anyway."

"Come now, Caleb."

"I'm tellin' the truth! A friend of mine—well, he's kind of a friend—he all the sudden said he didn't want them anymore but couldn't get rid of them at his place."

"Who is this friend?"

"I don't want to say. Anyway, he passed them on to me. I kind of forgot about them."

"Really?" She doubted any such "friend" had given Caleb the cigarettes. No, he'd just been caught.

"Really." His eyes blazed, daring her to doubt him. "I didn't want them, but my friend made me take them in order to throw them away. I didn't feel like I had a choice." He paused. Looked at her with wide eyes. "Have you ever felt like that?"

She nodded. Of course she knew. Everyone faced situations like that. When she'd gone to Indiana to see Malcolm, she'd known right away that he wasn't the one for her. Yet she stayed. It would have been most embarrassing to admit such a mistake . . . when she'd begged and pleaded to go for weeks beforehand. Of course by then Katie and Jonathan had fallen in love, so her going to Indiana had served a purpose in the end.

"My parents aren't home right now, you know," he said quickly. "They're in Lancaster. All that's home is Eli and now Sam, and I don't know what they'd say. I'd just rather they not find out, you know?"

"I understand. It's one thing to have to answer to parents, another when it's an older brother."

"They say things like they understand, but they're different than me. Neither of them ever wanted just to goof off for a little bit."

"Instead of worrying about who I'm going to tell, I think you should tell me the whole story."

He kicked the wheel of his buggy, causing his horse to snort in annoyance. "What do you mean? They're just cigarettes—not drugs. I wasn't doing anything too bad."

Winnie treaded carefully. "You know . . . some-times accidents can happen. Things can happen when we don't even mean for them to."

Caleb bit his lip. "I know that."

What did he know? "So, where has this boy you know been smoking?"

"I don't know."

"Are you sure? Maybe he's been sneaking around. At night? Maybe he's been going to other people's places?"

"I don't—" His eyes widened. "What are you asking?"

"Nothing," she replied, back-pedaling fast. She'd wanted Caleb to confess to his part in the fire, not rely on her to coax it out of him.

And what if she was wrong about everything?

"Never mind. Like I said, I promise I won't tell your parents."

*"Danke,"* he said with a nod, then turned away.

Well, she wasn't lying—she wasn't going to tell his parents a thing. But she was going to tell Eli. He needed to know what his brother was doing.

And even if it was all innocent, it wasn't her place to guess what needed to be done.

Pointing to the smashed box of cigarettes, he mumbled, "I'll get rid of these soon."

"The sooner the better, yes?"

Caleb didn't answer.

Sam couldn't deny it, he couldn't stop thinking about Winnie Lundy. Every time he'd been in her company, he'd found himself sneaking glances at her every chance he could get. He found her smooth black hair intriguing. And those dimples delighted him just enough to want to encourage her to smile as often as possible.

He liked her spunk, too. Sam knew more than one woman who would not have bounced back from injuries as well as Winnie Lundy did. No, she was no meek miss.

Yes, he'd thought quite a bit about Winnie, and about living Amish while he was back at home. Helping to plow fields and put into practice some of his agricultural theories had been a treat as well.

As had being close to Caleb.

But then he'd gone back to his real life. He slept in his apartment, watched ESPN, and worked non-stop. But nothing seemed the same.

Yes, he'd seen her that time he went to the Lundys' for meatloaf. He'd also talked to her when she'd called.

But it wasn't enough.

And though his feelings for her worried him, he found that he didn't want to push her away from his thoughts. No, he liked thinking about her. Liked seeing her. And he needed to see her again. Needed it as much as heirloom tomatoes needed good fertilizer.

Free from responsibilities, on Saturday morning he drove back to the small area of stores in the out-skirts of Peebles and found the antique shop where Winnie had recently started working again.

After parking in the gravel lot around the corner, Sam walked in, then felt like a bull in a china shop . . . or what he was—a large man in a flowery, cramped jumble of breakable items.

The place set his teeth on edge.

Then he spied her. A wrinkle had settled in between Winnie's expressive eyes as she counted a bunch of tiny porcelain thimbles on the counter in front of her. Yet still . . . she looked as pretty as ever.

Her head snapped up when he knocked into a rickety picture frame. "Sam?"

"Winnie," he said, just as calm as could be. It was a pleasure to watch the range of emotions cross her expression. She went from harried to shocked to pleased to . . . he wasn't sure what. The wide-eyed expression on her face was definitely something he would always be glad he saw, it was almost comical.

Oh, Winnie Lundy lightened his day just by being herself. He was terribly glad he'd decided to come see her.

Finally, she spoke. "Is everything all right?" Lumbering to her feet, she scanned his face. "Are the girls sick? Katie?"

He motioned for her to rest herself. "Everyone's fine, Win. Sit down, now, before you hurt your foot."

"Then why . . . why are you here?"

Of course she would ask the obvious. That was Winnie's way, no mincing words for her! Feeling vaguely embarrassed, he answered her. "I just thought I'd pay you a visit today and maybe see if you would have time to go to lunch." Yes. Lunch. Food was always a good idea.

Even in the dim light, Sam noticed her cheeks pinken. "Oh. I'm sorry. I . . . I brought my lunch."

"Oh." Was that how it was, then? He'd mistaken their burgeoning friendship to mean far more to her than it did? "Well, then, I guess I'll just look around, then."

She opened her mouth, shut it, then nodded.

He was left to wander around the place and try not to knock into things. He felt like a clumsy fool.

From the back room, an elderly lady spied him and approached, her gray dress almost fading in with some of the washed-out upholstery of two sofas. "May I help you?"

"No. I, um, was just looking around."

A gleam flickered in her narrow eyes. "For something special, perhaps?" She picked up a monstrous china pear. "Fruit makes nice gifts."

He couldn't imagine a worse item to receive. "Surely?"

"Oh, yes. It's not something one would buy for oneself."

He was stuck in the conversation and he couldn't get out. "*Jah*. I mean, yes, I can see that."

Winnie blurted, "He's with me, Madeline."

"Ah." Sizing him up, the small woman looked him up and down. "Perhaps you came here looking for something special after all, hmm?"

"I only stopped by for a moment." He backed toward the door.

"You don't have to leave right away, Samuel," Winnie said.

"Oh?" There'd been a hint of sweetness in her

voice. Maybe things weren't as awkward as he'd feared?

He shifted his weight for a moment back and forth, then was thankful when the owner shuffled off toward the back and they were alone again. He looked for something to say. "So, how's business today?"

"Slow."

"Oh. I'm sorry."

"I don't mind too much, not really. It's my first day back and all."

"I thought you were going to try and rest." Remembering how stern the nurse's instructions had been, he murmured, "You should've listened."

"I have been resting. But it was time to go to work." Winnie slowly got to her feet. "Madeline?" she called out. "Would you mind so much if I took a break?"

As quick as lightning, the lady poked her head out of the back room again. "No. Take your time, Winifred. Be careful, please. Don't want to knock over the merchandise."

Sam stepped forward. "I'll be glad to help you out of here." Anything to leave the claustrophobic environment!

*"Danke,"* she murmured.

Now that he felt in charge again, Sam curved a hand around her waist before she had time to move away. "Make your way slowly, and I'll be here for you in case you fall." Lowering his voice, he murmured, "I'm far more worried about your neck than ugly fruit."

Winnie fought off a giggle. Then she concentrated on fighting off other feelings—such as the tingle she felt from Sam's hand around her waist.

Or how special she'd felt when he'd said those wonderful words. *I'll be here for you.*

As she felt the heat from his hand coax through the fabric, making her warm and toasty, she hopped a little bit faster through the mixed up maze. "I don't know what we're going to do when I don't need your help anymore."

"Hopefully, we'll think of something."

His voice was gravelly and sure, not teasing at all. Which, of course, made her even more jumpy and light-headed. Winnie hobbled forward, knocking into a pair of baskets and a wooden hand-carved train. "Oh!" Perhaps she should've gotten her crutches.

Out from nowhere was his steady presence again. Keeping her safe and secure. One hand gripped her waist, the other righted the baskets. "Easy, now."

"I'm not usually so clumsy."

"I know." Lowering his voice, he murmured, "You're not clumsy, Winnie. Not by a long shot."

There was something in his voice that made her look at him quickly, but Sam's expression was almost serene as he curved one hand around her elbow to help her exit the building and make their way down the cobblestone path. "Want to sit for a moment?"

"Sitting sounds wonderful—*gut*." In no time Winnie was on a wooden park bench by Sam's side. "It is *shnokk* here, don'tcha think?"

Sam's eyes widened. "Cute? Well, hmm. Yes, I suppose it is."

As usual the charming town was bustling and busy. All around them, shoppers and tourists were chatting, eating waffle cones, carting boxes of fresh Amish baked goods, and talking on cell phones.

Though no one was rude enough to try and photograph her, Winnie was particularly aware of her dress and how obvious their differences were as she and Sam sat side by side.

Since he was saying nothing, she murmured, "I, um, I'm sorry if I seemed discourteous when you first entered. I was just surprised, is all."

"No, I should've warned you that I was thinking about stopping by."

Remembering his hurt expression about passing up lunch, she said, "And lunch—going out to lunch would be mighty nice. Another time."

"Yes. Maybe another time."

He sounded so doubtful; she did her best to be encouraging. "If you're out this way again, lunch would be a treat. If . . . If you'd still care to um, eat."

"I imagine I'll want to eat lunch another day."

Now that she finally saw his smile and heard his humor, Winnie relaxed. "Tell me a story from your week, Sam. I want to get back to how we used to be. I don't care much for this stilted, strained conversation."

"Gladly. Would you like to hear about my parents' latest letter? It seems that my grandparents' health has really improved. They'll be starting home before too long."

Relaxing against the back of the bench, Winnie nodded. "I'd love to hear about your family, Samuel."

And so, Sam talked. Winnie listened, but also daydreamed at the same time. And, against her better instincts, she wondered what a future by his side could be like. If it was even possible.

Because at the moment, Winnie didn't know if she'd ever felt happier than she did right then—sitting in the sun with a broken foot, all while talking about families and work and nothing at all.

Perhaps God really did answer prayers.

# Chapter 13

Caleb kicked the milk pail. As his thick-soled boot hit the metal brim, fresh milk splattered everywhere, speckling the packed earth underfoot and the sides of the thick fencing with white dots.

For one startling moment, the three Miller brothers stared in disbelief at the terrible mess.

"I didn't mean to do that," Caleb said.

"I'm sure you did," Sam replied. "Otherwise you wouldn't have launched your foot at the pail." Looking their little brother up and down, he added, "I sure am glad I came out here this weekend to help some more. Eli shouldn't have to deal with your tantrums on his own."

"I am not having a tantrum."

"You are certainly not doing anything good. I have to tell ya, Caleb, I expected more from you."

Caleb puffed up a bit, definitely in a huff. "Well, I expected to be trusted."

"We don't always get what we want, now, do we?" Looking as mad as a hornet, Eli pointed to the milky mess. "You're going to have to clean every bit of this up, and sanitize the bucket, too. We don't have time for such *dumhayda*, such foolishness. We have work to do, don't you remember?"

Scowling, Caleb said, "Of course, I remember. All I ever do is chores. It's you two who seem to find time for other things."

Sam had had enough of the tantrum. "Such as?"

Crossing his arms over his chest, Caleb replied, "Things like sneaking around and watching me."

Eli shook his head. "I wasna sneaking, Caleb."

"Oh, yes, you were! You were watching me and talking to Winnie Lundy about me—and thinking things. I canna believe you thought I would knowingly burn down the Lundys' barn."

"No one has accused you," Sam pointed out.

"Sure you did. Well, you were going to."

Eli groaned. "Caleb—you shouldn't have been listening to other people's—"

"You shouldn't have been saying such things!"

"Enough." Sam knew it was time to try and bring a bit of calm into the situation. It wasn't going to be easy. Ever since Caleb had overheard them speculating about his involvement in the fire, things had gone downhill fast. "We all need to calm down and talk this through."

"I don't want to." Bright red splotches of anger formed on Caleb's cheeks. "I wish Mamm and Daed were here. They'd tell you how wrong you were." His chin lifted. "They would."

Eli glared. "I wish they were, too. Because then you probably wouldn't have pulled half the things you've done this spring."

Back went the obstinate look. "Like what?"

"Like staying out late. Lying about your where-abouts."

Kicking the ground, Caleb said, "I don't want to be ganged up against."

"Then don't ruin a day's milk, *bruder*."

"Look. I know I made a mess. But, that doesn't mean I set fires."

Eli leaned his head against one of the stable doors. "You are not listening."

Grabbing Caleb's shoulder, Sam gently squeezed. "Just listen, will ya? You can't live your life in separate lanes, like on the hills around us, Caleb," Sam cautioned. "Things don't move on their own, parallel. They mix together, influencing each other. Your actions of late have cast doubts. We didn't blame you, but I'd be lying if I said we didn't feel like we needed to ask you about the fire."

"And we were going to," Eli said.

"Only after I heard you talking about me."

Eli sighed. "This discussion is the reason I was reluctant to ask you about things. I was worried you'd get all hotheaded."

Turning to Sam, Caleb's eyes filled with tears. "Sam, I thought you liked me."

"I do."

"Then why won't you believe me? I promise I'm not lying."

Sam's heart broke as he pulled his kid brother in for a hug. No, they hadn't handled this conversation well at all. Neither he nor Eli had a woman's knack for tact. Winnie would've known what to say. And well, Caleb was right. Their parents were far better at dealing with conflicts. They did have six *kinner*, after all.

Nestled against Sam's chest, Caleb's body shook. "You did say things could be separate. Like how you were Amish in your heart even though you went out into the world."

This time it was Sam who felt Eli's curious glare. Now, though, Sam was beginning to realize that "separate" wasn't how he could live his life after all. Slowly, he spoke, verbalizing his thoughts the moment they became clear in his mind. "I was wrong."

"What?"

"I wanted to learn when I was your age. I wanted something different than what I already had. And it made me feel ashamed. No, it wasn't driving cars or smoking or staying out late. But it was different, and I wanted it badly. Mamm and Daed understood my feelings and let me go live with the Johnsons. I was so relieved."

As he caught Eli's interested gaze, Sam realized that he'd never shared these inner feelings with his older brother either.

His desire not to hurt anyone's feelings had backfired. Instead of creating an aura of peace, it had only instilled a fair amount of distrust and confusion.

Thinking back, Sam felt driven to confess everything completely. "Being away from here was hard. As I studied for my GED, I tried to cling to our ways and still fit in with all the *Englischers*. I stayed in my clothes, hugged my beliefs tightly. But then . . . I began to feel too different. I wanted to learn so badly, I put that first and began to adopt some of the Johnsons' ways." With a helpless shrug, he added, "It was easier to get along."

This time it was Eli who did the reaching out. With a pat on his arm, he murmured, "Do not be so hard on yourself, Samuel. You were only sixteen, after all. That's not so old. And everyone likes to fit in."

Sam shared a smile with Caleb. "*Jah*, Caleb. I was only sixteen."

Caleb looked at him suspiciously. "What's that smile supposed to mean?"

"It means that at sixteen, I, too, thought I knew so much. But sometimes I still made mistakes, just like I do now."

"Back then, what did you do?"

"I prayed. I clung to my belief in Christ. But I let the conveniences influence me, same as anything else. I moved on, away from our ways."

"But you're a fancy *Englischer* now—a college professor. Everyone says you're a smart man and is proud of you. Why do you think you did something wrong?"

"Because I tried to live my life in a narrow path,

thinking I could have everything if I only looked straight ahead, never side to side. But that was a foolhardy thing to do. We're all connected to each other, Caleb. The Lord lets us live in communities because we need them. For too long, I tried to excuse my behavior by thinking that it was okay for me to ignore some of our rules, because the Lord had gifted me with a strong desire to learn."

"And a really large brain."

Eli chuckled. "But now you think you are not fitting in?"

"Now I see what I have given up to reach for my dreams. I haven't been here for you, Caleb. I haven't been here for Eli or our parents." He also hadn't been around for Winnie, and had a feeling that if he had had her steady, bright influence, his world might have run more smoothly.

Eli cleared his throat. "Caleb, since we are now certain you did not start the fire, I have a terribly important question to ask you."

Those golden eyes of his blinked. "Yes?"

"Do you know who did?"

After two eternal minutes, Caleb nodded slowly. "I think so. But I don't know why."

"You need to tell us who. Jonathan Lundy needs to know the truth."

"First—I've gotta ask you something."

"Yes?"

"Would either of you mind if I only told Jonathan?"

171

Sam was shocked. "You don't want to tell us?"

"No."

Eli scowled. "You don't trust us now?"

"I trust you, but I know this friend of mine trusted me." Looking away, he said, "I know I need to betray his confidence. But if I'm going to do this, I'd rather only tell the one person who needs to know."

"And it's not us," Sam said with a knowing look to Eli.

"Are you mad?" Caleb asked.

"No. If I'm honest, I'm right proud of you," Eli replied. "You, little brother, have just grown up. Do you want me to take you to Jonathan's tonight, or do you want to go on your own?"

With a new resolve in his features, Caleb shook his head. "I'll go on my own. Now that we've talked . . . I think I'm finally ready to accept responsibility."

Sam looked at Eli and felt as old as the hills. "We'll be here waiting, then. Waiting and praying."

"But first," Eli said with a raised brow. "First, it's time to clean up your mess. Yes?"

With a sigh, Caleb reached for the bucket. "Yes."


"I am thankful you could come help me with this work, Caleb," Jonathan said to the teen when he'd shown up late in the afternoon unexpectedly. All he'd said was that he wanted to help with the barn for a bit. Guessing that far more was on his mind, Jonathan nodded, slipped on his work gloves and led Caleb to what was left of the pile of burnt lumber.

Now, as they worked hard together, Jonathan prayed that he and Caleb would eventually get to the real reason for his visit. And that he would listen with a bit more patience and tact than was his usual habit. However, his insides were raging and impatient. All he wanted to do was let loose of the crazy mesh of emotions that had been rolling inside of him from the moment he'd heard the first snap of burning wood.

Pulling out a partially burned board and tossing it into the scrap pile with a grunt, Caleb merely nodded.

"I am going to need a lot of help prepping this area, especially if it is going to be ready for the barn raising."

"What are you going to do with all the wood?"

"Burn it. Not much else it's good for."

With a sideways look, Jonathan added, "You know, it's a terrible shame that this even happened. All from someone's carelessness."

Caleb's hands stilled. "Mr. Lundy, that's why I came here. I need to talk to you about that."

"Oh?"

"See . . . well—are you sure you need to know who started the fire?"

"I think I do. While I'm putting the Lord firmly

in charge of things, I feel a need to know. A need to understand." He glanced Caleb's way to make sure he was listening. "See, it looks like a spark from a cigarette created all this destruction. Something so small changed everything in one minute. Right while I was sleeping. I pulled my sister out right about here." He pointed to the spot where the barn's doors used to lay. "Caleb, if the Lord hadn't put me here, she might have died. It's hard to come to grips with something like that."

Caleb swallowed. "What do you mean, come to grips with?"

"To realize that through someone's honest mistake, my sister could have been taken from me."

"But it was just an accident."

"But we need to take responsibility even if something was unintentional. Though I'm ashamed to admit it, it's these things that keep me up at night. I'm trying to forgive, but my heart isn't ready until I have someone to forgive."

"What are you going to do?"

"I'm going to keep hoping and praying and watching. Maybe one day I will know who was responsible."

Caleb picked up another two boards and laid them on the pile. When he picked up another piece of wood, a good portion of it crumbled under his fingertips. As the black ash flew to the ground, the boy looked troubled.

"Careful, now," Jonathan said. "This looks like

just wood, but there's nails and things around here. If we're not careful, we're going to get cut."

"I've got gloves on." The boy held up two hands to prove his point.

"Gloves don't protect you from everything. That's why the Lord gave us a mind, don'tcha think? We need to use it every now and then."

"Jonathan . . . if you do find out who burned your barn, what are you going to do to him?"

"I don't know. Talk to him, I suspect."

"That's pretty dumb. Talking doesn't help."

"It might help me, though." He caught the boy's eye. "I'm thinkin' if someone is able to come forward and talk to me about the fire, about what happened, it might help a lot. A conversation can be pretty powerful." With a shrug, Jonathan lifted another board and added it to the pile. "Of course, we both know that no one has come to talk to me. I wish that wasna the case, though."

"Maybe the person was scared."

"I suspect he was. Or *she* was. Of course, I was scared too, that night. Ach." With a grimace, Jonathan pulled a nail out of the thick leather of his glove.

"Did you get hurt?"

"Not badly. Just a prick."

Caleb visibly tried to measure a smile. "I heard that we're supposed to be real careful with the boards. There might be nails and such."

"I heard boys are supposed to watch their mouths

around their elders." Jonathan found himself also doing his best to temper his smile.

"I'm trying."

Patting the boy on the shoulder, Jonathan murmured, "So, is that what you wanted to talk about?"

"Kind of." Caleb closed his eyes for a moment then with a lost, helpless look, murmured, "I think I know who set the fire."

"Who do you think it might be?"

"David Hostetler. He's been acting nervous and such. He also handed me some cigarettes and asked me to get rid of them. He acted like he was scared to even touch them." Golden eyes watering, Caleb said, "I never wanted to tell on him, but my brothers started thinking that it might have been me."

It took every bit of effort for Jonathan to keep his expression neutral and easy. For him not to start peppering Caleb with a dozen questions. "I'm sure that bothered you."

"It did. Verra much. I'd rather be in trouble for the truth, you know? Only the truth can help sometimes."

"I think you're right about that." He held out his hand and shook Caleb's. "I'll keep this to myself for a bit. I appreciate you coming here and telling me."

"I hope it was the right thing."

"I know it was. No one ever promised that the

right thing would always feel good. Sometimes the right thing just lets you sleep at night."

After Caleb left, Jonathan walked out beyond the remains of the barn, away from the house. He needed a moment to come to grips with what he'd just learned.

So . . . David Hostetler.

He always liked the boy. He felt a bit sorry for his home life. He was such a shy, timid thing, too. In his heart, Jonathan figured if it had been David, he must have been scared to death.

Frightened.

Alone.

That knowledge caught Jonathan off guard. He'd been hugging his anger to his chest like a shield. And consequently, that anger had prevented him from thinking about how anyone else might have been feeling. That knowledge shamed him.

It was time to *fagebb*, to forgive. And, he realized, the Lord was asking him to do something harder, too. Instead of waiting for someone to take the blame, he was going to need to reach out to David. Reach out and lend a hand. And hope it was the right thing to do.

# Chapter 14

"It was kind of you to pick me up after my doctor's appointment again," Winnie said to Samuel after he helped her navigate her way from the medical building and into the large cab of his black Ford truck.

"You should have asked me to come pick you up from home and take you here, too," he chided as soon as he moved into the cab beside her and buckled up. "I would have been happy to do that."

"It was no bother hiring a driver. I don't want to take advantage of you." She'd also been hesitant about spending so much time alone with him. The feelings she had for Samuel Miller seemed to become stronger with each passing day. And though she could envision a life with him one day, she still wasn't sure if he was on the same page, or just helping out a family friend.

"You're never a bother, Win."

Winnie shifted in her seat. It was a somewhat jerky move, what with the new cast on her foot. But hopefully, it wouldn't be on for much longer. The doctor had examined her most recent set of X rays and proclaimed her to be healing nicely. Her new cast was smaller and lighter and now allowed her to bear a bit of weight on it. "I'm so happy to be more mobile," she said.

"I hope you don't overdo it."

"I won't. Besides, I'd rather have sore arms from hopping around on crutches than continue to feel isolated. I didn't care for that one bit."

"I bet you didn't. I can't imagine you ever being happy to sit on the sidelines."

"That would be me, for better or worse."

"Now that you've gone to the doctor, where would you like to go now?" He grinned. "I am at your mercy."

Winnie blinked. Oh, when he said things like that, he almost sounded like he was in a courting frame of mind. But she knew he wasn't really. Playing it safe, she said, "I don't care. We can just go home, if you'd like."

"I'll take you home." He paused. "I have to make a stop first, though. Are you in a hurry?"

"Not at all." He smiled at her blunt answer, right about the time when she wished she'd have learned to watch her boldness.

"I have to stop by my office, but then I was hoping you might like to get a bite to eat."

A smarter woman would be more watchful of her heart. But no matter what her brain might be telling her, she couldn't ignore her heart—being in Sam's company made her happy. "Yes, let's go to your office. I've been curious about your place of work."

"All right, then." With a few turns, Sam pulled into the parking lot in front of a wide array of red-bricked buildings. "This is where I work. There are some benches outside; I can walk you over to one while I run to my office."

"Is your office on the second floor?"

"No, it's on the first."

"Then, I'd like to go inside and see what you do."

"It's not fancy," he warned.

"Good. I'm not fancy either." She felt deliciously warm when he smiled at her joke.

Looking a bit awkward, Sam finally nodded. "All right, then. Off we go."

He helped her out of the car, then led the way. Students were everywhere. Two girls looked at her curiously, then walked on the grass so she could continue on the sidewalk. Winnie gave them a friendly smile.

Everywhere she looked, Winnie spied something new and interesting. Each building they passed was constructed of dark red brick, black-trim framed windows. Matching black doors marked each entry.

Gardeners had been busy. Flower beds of cheery begonias and brightly colored petunias decorated the spaces between the buildings. And then there were the statues. Every few yards, another bronze figure dotted the landscape. She stopped in front of the one closest to them. "Who's he?" she asked.

"I don't recall exactly. He's one of the founders of the school. There are statues all around the campus."

"It's a remarkable place," Winnie murmured. Everyone looked so interesting and studious. "This is where you went to college, yes?"

"Yes. They gave me a full scholarship." Looking around fondly, Sam stopped for a moment. "I'm glad you're here, Winnie. For somehow I've started to only think of this campus as my place of work. I forgot all about my first impressions."

Sam clasped her elbow as they approached the two wide cement stairs that led up to the main doorway. "Have a care, now," he murmured as she struggled to find just the right place to position the ends of her crutches.

He hovered around her, making sure she was stable, then curved an arm around her side to help prop open the door.

When they went in, Winnie caught a glimpse of two bulletin boards before being ushered into a musty-smelling office.

Right away a voice greeted them. "Professor Miller?"

"Afternoon, Zach." With a smile, Winnie turned to the man. But for a moment, she couldn't help but stare at him. He had multiple piercings in his eyebrows and one circular silver loop on one of his lips. But what was most surprising was his hair—it was a short, spiky bright red—the color of watermelon in July.

To her surprise, he was staring back at her with just as much curiosity and interest. "Who are you?"

"Winnie Lundy."

"Hi. Hey, I like your hat."

"Thank you." Cautiously, Winnie touched her *kapp* to make sure all her hair was still neatly in place.

Sam stepped in between them, breaking the inspections. "Zach, Winnie is a friend of mine from back home. Winnie, please meet Zach Crawford. He helps me try and keep this place organized."

"Hello," she said, nodding her head.

Zach darted a look of amusement toward Sam. "Did you grow up with Professor Miller?"

*"Jah."*

*"Jah?"* A smile passed over Zach's face. "I love your accent. So, you two are friends, huh? What was he like as a kid? Super smart? A know-it-all?"

"I'm not sure what a know-it-all means, but he was always terribly *shmeaht*, I mean, smart. Even when we were in school together."

"No kidding? I didn't think you two were the same age."

"Oh, Samuel's older, but we Amish have many grades in one building."

"Like in the olden days, huh? Was it hard to—"

Sam rapped his knuckles on Zach's desk. "That's enough questions for now, don't you think?"

"Oh! Yeah, sure." Nodding toward Winnie's pale cast and crutches, Zach said, "Hey, I'm sorry about your leg."

*"Danke."*

"How'd you break it? Driving a buggy?"

"Zach . . ." Sam's voice held a warning. Winnie wondered what, exactly, he was warning his assistant about. Because they were speaking to each other so much?

When she looked his way, she understood. "I'm sorry for all the questions," he said with a concerned expression.

"I don't mind." When she turned toward Zach again, she was amused to see him now leaning on the desk, his chin resting in his hands. His attention was focused on her, and his expression was filled with honest curiosity, not anything mean-hearted.

"I hurt my leg in a fire," she said. "A bad one."

"No way." Zach's eyes widened. "Where was it? Your house?"

"Oh, no. It was in our barn, in the middle of the night. I hurt myself trying to get some goats out."

"Wow! I never met anyone who raised goats."

"They're *gut* pets, I'll tell you that. But they are ornery and eat most anything."

"I've heard that. My cousin raised pigs. Now, they do eat everything. My cousin Jamie said they got out and ate a whole Jell-o salad. Their noses were bright red!"

Winnie chuckled. "Zach, a *pikk's naws*, I mean a pig's nose would be a snout, *jah*?"

"Oh. *Jah*."

Sam rolled his eyes. "I only came in here to check on some things. We won't be long."

But Zach didn't seem to care about his schedule at all. "There are some notes for you right here," he muttered, before turning back to Winnie. "How did you put out the flames? Blankets? Buckets of water?"

"Ach, no! The fire trucks came, of course."

"I didn't know you all used the fire department."

"Oh, sure. We Amish use the fire department, just as anyone. We've all helped put out fires, too. We like to help each other, you know?"

"That's nice." Pointing to her leg, he said, "But you still got hurt?"

"Yes. A board or somethin' knocked me out and my *bruder* Jonathan had to pull me to freedom. The whole episode was scary, I'll tell you that."

Sam threw up his hands and walked away. "I think I'll bow out of this conversation while I can. I'll be right back, Winnie."

"Have a seat," Zach offered, not looking dismayed in the slightest by the way Sam had spoken to him. "Would you like a cup of tea or a glass of water?"

"Yes, *danke*."

Zach looked delighted to hear her speak. "*Danke?* Does that mean thank you?"

Sam poked his head out of his office door. "It does. Winnie, you don't have to drink anything."

"I can speak for myself, Samuel. It is my leg that's hurt, not my mouth."

184

His own straightened into a thin line. "Obviously."

Oh! Why was he acting so strange? Was he nervous for her to find out things about his life at the university . . . or for Zach to find out things about his past?

Zach brought her a glass of water, which she sipped on just as the phone started ringing and a crowd of students blew in the door.

And *blew* was exactly what their arrival seemed like! The group of four boys and three young women were loud and boisterous, and moved in a pack. Each one was wearing a combination of shorts and T-shirt, some with big, clunky sandals . . . others with tennis shoes.

With barely a look in her or Zach's direction— who was on the phone and writing down notes anyway—they rushed toward Sam's door.

And then Winnie got a real opportunity to see what Sam's life at school was really like. Without even a pause at the threshold, they scampered through the opening and almost without drawing a breath, peppered him with questions.

Across from her, Zach turned away and started typing something on his computer, still talking on the phone. The kids, obviously vying for immediate attention, just kept getting louder and louder. They shot questions Sam's way that Winnie didn't understand.

It all sounded very foreign and yet exciting.

Winnie sipped her water and just listened to the commotion around her. Just as Zach lowered the phone, it rang again. The door opened and shut, and more students wandered in and out. Somehow they'd all known that Professor Miller had arrived and were obviously glad to see him.

Sam, for his part, seemed to treat them all with the resigned patience of a put-upon big brother, offering advice and instructions with humor and a touch of steel.

Now she understood the choices he'd made. A college setting was where he belonged.

After a good thirty minutes, Sam ducked out of his office again, looking sheepish. "I'm sorry, I never intended for this to take so long."

"I enjoyed sitting here and watching everything. It's lively."

To Sam's dismay, Zach let out a bark of laughter. "It's always this way when Professor Miller is here."

"Why is that?"

"He's a popular professor. Always has time for the students, which they really appreciate. And he's so amazingly quick and smart. He reads all the latest journals and studies and can analyze their pros and cons really fast."

"That's wonderful—*gut*, Samuel, *jah*?"

"Zach's making more of me than he needs to." Carrying a satchel stuffed with a bunch of blue packets on one shoulder, Sam bent down to help

Winnie with her crutches. "Let's get you on home."

"Hope you'll come back and visit, Winnie."

"*Danke,* Zach. I'm sure I shall. It was good to meet you."

Zach was still beaming when Sam escorted her slowly out the door. After negotiating herself down the stairs with Sam wrapping a hand around her waist in case she lost her bearings, she turned to Sam. "This was fun."

"I'm glad you visited. Would you still like to grab something to eat before we head on back?"

"Sure." As she approached his truck, she wondered what his life was going to be like years from now. Would he ever find a woman who would make him happy? Would he one day settle down here, forever?

The thought of Samuel once again having a life she was not a part of made her blue. She'd miss him something awful.

When he opened his truck door, she gratefully accepted his help getting in.

"Winnie, are you okay?" he asked just before he closed her door. "You look like you're about to cry."

"Oh, it's nothing. I was just thinkin' about how different our lives are."

"Not so different, not really. Inside, I'm still the same Samuel Miller you used to play basketball with."

"We're different enough. I'm Amish. You are not."

A muscle in his jaw jumped. "That is true."

Winnie's outspoken nature got the best of her again. It hurt too much to keep everything she was thinking inside. "Sometimes when I think about you gettin' married and staying here, away from our community, it makes me sad, Samuel."

For a moment, he looked stunned. Finally, he spoke up. "The truth is, Winnie, when I think about that, I get sad, too."

"Truly?"

He nodded. "But see, inside, in my heart, I just don't see myself getting married here. It's not going to happen."

Not going to happen. His pronouncement felt like a crushing blow. He wasn't thinking about marriage? Ever?

And here she'd thought she'd come to mean a lot to him. She'd completely misread his feelings— and she'd done just what she'd been trying not to do—imagine the two of them with a life together.

"I actually have been . . ."

But she'd heard enough. "If you don't mind, I think we better get on home. I betcha Katie could use some help watching the girls."

"Don't you want to get some lunch? We could talk some more . . ."

"No. I'm not too hungry. And . . . I'm kind of tired, too."

"Did I say something to upset you?"

Oh, she yearned to tell him everything. How she'd been thinking about him so, so much. How she desperately wanted things to work out for them, one way or another. But at the moment, it was terribly obvious that could never happen.

"Of course not. You've been a wonderful *friend*, driving me around. I'm grateful for your friendship."

"All right, then," he murmured, not looking too happy.

Winnie pretended to sleep the rest of the way home. It was easier than pretending her heart wasn't breaking.

She couldn't deny anymore that she'd really begun to hope that they might've had a future together. For a little while, she thought maybe they had a chance. Instead, all that happened was that she'd gotten her heart broken again.

# Chapter 15

Sam didn't understand what had happened. One minute, Winnie was excited about visiting the university and his life. The next, she was talking about him being married. When he'd tried to ease her worries, she'd just looked hurt and disappointed.

"She was near impossible, Eli," he complained, practically the moment he walked into the kitchen.

Looking up from his plate of baked chicken, canned fruit, and carrots, Eli looked confused, "Who is?"

"Winnie. I don't know what she wants." He held up a hand to stop the incoming question. "And before you ask if I asked her, I did. Asking for her to explain herself didn't help."

Pulling his plate toward him, Eli grunted. "I see."

"Do you?" From the moment Sam had entered Eli's home and interrupted his supper, he'd been talking up a storm. What a change from their usual routine. Now it was Eli who was doing the nodding and Sam who was pacing and running his mouth.

Eli pushed back his chair and walked across the kitchen to wash his plate and neatly set it in the drying rack. After that, Eli pulled open the back door and led Sam outside.

Together they walked out toward the edge of one

of the fields. Sam shared a smile with his brother when they saw their accomplishment. In the fading sun, rows and rows of freshly tilled soil lay before them. It had taken days of hard work to prepare the land for planting, but now it looked beautiful to Sam's eyes. There was something about land that had been cared for that gave it a special look. Healthy and fresh.

He breathed deep, enjoying the scent of freshly tilled soil. Yes, it was a strange scent to enjoy, but it smelled wonderful to him. It was why no matter how much schooling he'd done—he needed the land as much as it needed him.

"So, Winnie Lundy's got your heart. That's an interesting thought."

Looking sideways at Eli, Sam commented, "You know, I never actually said that."

"Come now, Samuel."

"All right. Yes, I suppose she does have my heart, but there's nothing I can do about it."

"Why's that? She'd make any man a wonderful-*gut frau*."

"She would, but . . . I'd have to move back here. Do you think the Lord really guided me to all that learnin' just to travel back here?" To Sam, that seemed kind of a waste of time, though he supposed that was putting things a little harsh.

"But the two of you would make a good go of it. Perhaps she's your reason to come back to us," Eli stated practically.

"Everything isn't so easy. I'm a college professor, remember?"

"I haven't forgotten."

Something in the way Eli said that made Sam wonder if maybe he'd concentrated too much on his job over the years and not enough on family and relationships. Feeling defensive, he murmured, "My work at the college is important to me. I can't help that."

"I know." Together they walked slowly back to the house. "Perhaps we could speak to the bishop. Maybe he would let you still work, at least sometimes. Then you could have Winnie and your college."

But that seemed wrong. It would be selfish to try—he'd be putting his schedule and needs before his family's or his faith.

Besides, Samuel knew that attempting to juggle both worlds and his job and the needs of a wife wasn't an option. The life on campus was too worldly, and seemed to be getting more so each day. Students came to college full of excitement and information about the newest, fastest ways to do things. In spite of his best intentions, he'd gotten caught up in their excitement.

In contrast, the restrictions of the Amish way of life would make a daily transition difficult at best. He could make himself sick by trying to do justice to each facet and most likely would never please both groups.

No, he'd have to quit his job and find something else.

But then would he be happy? And what about all the time and work he'd put into things? "I wish I was more like you, you know."

Eli looked taken aback. "Never wish that. You are the smartest man I know."

Sam felt humbled by Eli's honesty. He knew his brother didn't speak those words lightly. He, like their parents, had valued Sam's desire to further his education. "I might be book smart, but you are far smarter in the ways of the world."

"I'm only trying to do what is best today and leave the rest up to God. He'll guide me—and you, too, if you let him, Sam."

"I'm trying."

Eli started heading back to the house, pausing before he stepped in the door. "I think you need to talk to the Lord more than me. *Stop,* Samuel. Stop rushing and planning and doing and driving. Stop and pray and listen."

When had been the last time he'd prayed for longer than a minute or two? When had been the last time he'd sat in silence and used the time to contemplate his wants and needs and what the Lord wanted him to do?

In a daze, Sam wandered back into the house to his mother's *Sitzschtupp* and stood still for a moment, just taking time to look around. The walls were freshly painted a creamy white. An oak plaque decorated the area above the fireplace, listing his parents' marriage and each child's birth. On the opposite wall a large quilt hung. Its vibrant red, blue, and black triangles never failed to catch his eye and imagination.

To his dismay, Sam now realized yet another reason why the Amish didn't have televisions and radios and computers. All that noise and business was distracting.

Slowly, Sam relaxed against the smooth wooden back of the *shokkel shtool*, the rocking chair that rested to the right of the fireplace, and closed his eyes.

Please Lord, he prayed. Please help me find myself.

And though he never talked about it much, moving away from his home and community had been trying. Though he still found solace in the scriptures and privately held fast to his prayers and his personal relationship with the Lord, many other activities in his life had taken some adjusting to.

And, for better or worse, he had also celebrated them. He liked taking advantage of modern conveniences. Sometimes he thought he wouldn't be able to get through his day without his cell phone, yet alone his computer. If he left all that, he would be forced to give it up.

He'd also be putting a barrier in between himself and the outside world again. Oh, sure, he would keep his friendships, but he knew in his heart that they'd all soon drift apart. It was only natural to do so. They'd have different interests.

And then there was his education and his love of learning. Would he ever be able to turn his back on that? It seemed like it would be difficult to face himself or the Lord if he did that. Hadn't the Lord given him a wonderful mind to put to good use? Wouldn't it be a mistake to ignore his gifts?

He wasn't sure.

"Lord, I'm feeling afraid," he said aloud. Finally daring to admit what was in his heart. "I'm afraid to hope for a future with Winnie. I'm afraid to ask her to leave the order. I'm afraid to give up my current way of life."

Worse, Sam distrusted this new surge of emotions he was feeling. He'd become used to knowing what he believed and walking forward. He felt four years old again. In his sturdy brother's shadow, he sometimes felt as if he would never measure up. How could he, really? Eli always made the right thing look so easy.

He'd happily settled into the farming way of life as did their parents and grandparents. While not perfect, Eli had always seemed determined to do his best—and most of the time, that was certainly good enough.

Sam, on the other hand, had always somehow managed to fight his expectations. He still was struggling with doubts.

He was startled from his trance by Caleb. He rushed into the *Sitzschtupp* with a flurry of motion, like he always did, but this time it didn't seem to be his usual restless spirit guiding him. His eyes were red, like he'd been trying not to cry. Obviously hearing Caleb's clunky steps, Eli rushed in, too.

*"Sam? Eli?"*

"Caleb, what is it?" Sam asked.

"I need help from both of you."

Eli set his open palm on their younger brother's shoulder. "Of course. Sit down and we'll talk."

Sam vaguely recalled how their mother had always offered them a hot drink when they were upset. "Do you want some hot chocolate?" Eli snapped to face him, his look conveying his confusion. Sam simply shrugged. "Anything at all?"

Caleb shook his head. "I just need you both to listen."

"That's what we're doin'," Eli said.

Caleb raised a hand. "I mean to say . . . would ya hear me out before saying anything? I need to talk and be heard, not lectured."

Sam let Eli take the lead. And, as usual, he did not disappoint. Eli said, "Now what is it? Are you still worried about the fire and your friend?"

Sam liked how Eli deliberately didn't try to push Caleb.

Caleb nodded. "When we talked, I didn't want to tell you any names. I told you and I told myself it was because I trusted my friend—and I only wanted the person who needed to know to know. But now I'm starting to wonder if I'd made the wrong decision."

Sam looked at Eli, who shrugged. "That's a very important change. What brought it on?"

"When I spoke with Jonathan, his manner reminded me of our *daed*." He looked at both Sam and Eli. "You know how Daed doesna say much but you know he always listens? How no matter what he loves us and cares?"

Sam nodded. That description fit their father well. "Yes?"

"Jonathan's manner reminded me of how different my friend's father is. He's verra different. My friend never talks that way about his parents. He's afraid to make mistakes. He's afraid to talk to his *daed*. And now, I'm afraid to talk to him because I told on him." Their brother's eyes filled with tears again. "Now he has nobody."

A dozen thoughts filled Sam's head. There was no simple answer to ease Caleb's worries. But when he looked toward Eli, Sam relaxed. As usual, Eli didn't look flustered at all. Instead, he was patting Caleb's slender shoulders.

Then Eli spoke. "Let's pretend no one ever cared about who started the fire. What would you think then? Would keeping the secret be okay?"

"I don't know. It feels like a terribly hard burden."

"Did you chat with the Lord and ask for His help?"

"No."

"You might want to consider doing that, Caleb. Sam and I were just talking about how much He helps us . . . when we admit we're only mortal," Eli said.

Eyes wide, Caleb turned to Sam. "Praying helped you?"

"More than I can put into words," Sam said.

Eli winked. "That is sayin' something, wouldn't you agree? Our brother always seems to have words on his tongue I don't understand." Squeezing Caleb's shoulder, he said, "This time, I don't know how to advise you. I think you did the right thing. Lying and pretending you don't know something won't make problems disappear."

"But what happens when my friend finds out I told? He's going to be so mad."

"I guess he'll either be mad at you or will let you try and explain your reasons. Either way, know that I'm proud of you."

Caleb blinked. "You are? After everything I told you?"

"Of course. You're my brother."

Warily Caleb looked to Sam. In the pit of his stomach, Sam felt the same way. "I love you and am proud of you, too." Taking a risk, he said, "Caleb, at the moment, you and I are facing some big problems—too big to face by ourselves. I've been wondering where I belong. You've been wondering who to side with. We need to not forget that the Lord is always with us. We need to involve Him in our worries and fears. If we offer ourselves, He will help."

"You think?"

"I know." With a smile, Sam waved a hand. "God provided us with each other, yes? I don't think that was happenstance."

Later that night, after Eli and Caleb had gone to bed and he only had the cool evening for company, Sam reflected on how peaceful he had felt advising and being advised by his family. It was something he hadn't truly experienced in years. And he missed it.

He knew without a doubt that the Lord had been at his side, guiding him. Caleb needed him, and Eli was offering his support and opening up to him. He felt as if he'd just stepped into where he needed to be, for the first time in years.

Suddenly, all of the doubts he'd held on to about his place in the world became clear as day. This was where he belonged. Their tight-knit community, with all the friendships and gossip and worries, was as much a part of him as the hair on his head. He'd been a fool to try and distance himself from that.

It was time to return to his family and to his community. Now he just had to find a place to fit in.

He decided to wait to speak to Winnie about his

new revelations until things had gotten organized. No sense in worrying her until he could offer her a future.

But oh, he was looking forward to a future with Winnie. For the first time in a long time, everything felt right.

# Chapter 16

After tossing and turning for hours, Winnie gave up sleeping. She put on her robe and slippers then carefully hobbled down the hall by the light of the moon still resting high in the nighttime sky. Oh, but it did feel freeing to only need one crutch.

With a few well-placed rests and a sturdy oak banister for support, Winnie left the stuffy confines of the house and found refuge in the cool comfort of the front porch. Instead of choosing a rocking chair, she claimed the top step, just as she had for what seemed all her life. It was her favorite spot to find solace.

And that was what she most definitely needed at the moment. Her thoughts were too chilling and worrisome. She'd fallen in love with a man she didn't want to love. Well, with a man she was *afraid* to love.

She didn't know what to do. So she did what her mother had taught her, so many years ago. She prayed.

Closing her eyes, she said the Lord's Prayer, spoken from her heart, each verse speaking to her soul. Though sprawling fields reminded Winnie that she was only one of God's creatures in the vast world, she still felt as if He was listening for her.

"Dear God, help me know your will," she whis-

201

pered into the still, starry sky. "I feel so alone and confused."

Asking God's will was really all Winnie felt she could do anymore. After all, the last few weeks had most definitely been in the Lord's hands. She could not think of another explanation for why she was led to Sam—a man she'd not spent much time with until recently.

And the Lord had most definitely seen to it that they'd meet. She and Jonathan had both remarked how odd it was that she had been the one to break her foot and sustain burns when he'd been in and out of the burning barn so many times.

The hospital was near where Samuel worked. And because Sam's brother Eli was good friends with Jonathan, Samuel had felt honor-bound to visit her.

A nonbeliever might have called that a coincidence, but it was too much of a coincidence for her. No, God had meant for her and Sam to cross paths once again.

Winnie just wasn't sure why.

Was it to strengthen her faith? To give her a trial like so many women and men in the Bible?

If that was His will, well, Winnie had to say that she was sorely disappointed. She already did love the Lord and intentionally sought His guidance on a daily basis.

The recent turn of events felt like a cruel joke.

"Lord, I know I'm Amish. I love my family. I

love my dear nieces. But I know I've fallen in love with Sam, too. I don't understand why You brought us together when You knew that love would be wrong."

As her words flew into the air and seemed to dissipate the moment she said them, Winnie closed her eyes and tried to listen to a reply.

But—as she was afraid would happen—no reply seemed to be forthcoming. Frustrated, she spoke again. "What do you want for me to do? Leave everything I know and love?"

A dawning awareness flew through her. Was that His will? That she leave the order, too?

Perhaps Samuel needed an Amish wife in an English world. He needed her values and their common ways.

Plus, it wasn't like he'd strayed too, too far from their way of life. Yes, he had adopted many English ways, but he still believed in their sense of community, their faith, and their rules, despite bending a few of them.

Yes, that had to be it. She and Sam hadn't met again so he would leave all his accomplishments and join her. No, they met so that she could be his partner and helpmate. So she could be the person who knew and understood him in a community where so many did not.

The thought of shouldering that responsibility scared her. She didn't know if she was ready to leave everything she'd known to be with Samuel.

As the cool night air fanned her face, Winnie reflected some more. Perhaps leaving her own kind to be with Samuel was what love was? Didn't love mean putting another's needs before your own?

In her other relationships with friends and family, she'd always been the type of woman who noticed what wasn't right, noticed qualities in other people that she wished could be changed. She noticed flaws in appearances and flaws in character. Katie had commented more than once that her outspoken ways sometimes hurt people's feelings.

She'd certainly had a time with Malcolm's absent-minded ways toward her. She hadn't liked being taken for granted. Hadn't liked not being appreciated.

Now that she was wiser, Winnie knew she'd been realizing that Malcolm hadn't loved her any more than she'd loved him. In each other's company, it had been necessary to think about other things and other people, because what they had was never special at all.

With Sam it was different. From the time she'd seen him in the hospital, he'd struck her fancy. She'd thought about him for hours. She imagined what future conversations would be like and reviewed what past conversations had included.

And though things weren't always wonderful between them, they were exciting. And she appreciated their differences. Yes, she accepted Samuel Miller just the way he was. And she was grateful when he accepted her that way, too.

She was in love, and was willing to do whatever it took to be with the person she loved. She'd waited too long to find this. At the moment, it meant accepting that he needed to be with the English. That his students and his research were important to him. She could make sacrifices for him, then.

Standing up, Winnie felt almost joyous. Despite the fact that she still had to convince him that marriage was the right path for them. But she now knew she was willing to make this sacrifice for him.

Though it would fair break her heart.

Because, she realized as she opened the door and stepped inside the house, while Samuel had left with his family's blessing, she would not be seeing the same acceptance.

He'd left before he'd taken the vows of the Amish faith. Before he'd joined the church. She would be leaving after.

It made all the difference in the world. He had been loved and always accepted.

*She* would be shunned.

Suddenly, it felt as if everything was crashing down once again.

As tears pricked her eyes, Winnie limped to her room. "Oh, dear Lord, You certainly know how to bend us to your will, don'tcha? I hope You will not leave me. I have a feeling I am about to need You more than ever. Please stay with me, no matter where I am. No matter who I am. Please know that I only want to follow Your will, and I want to honor You by being the best woman I can be. At the moment, I really do believe that the best thing for me is to be with Sam."

There was no turning back. She was frightened and nervous of her decision, but also felt curiously lighter. Even if nothing ever happened between her and Samuel, at least she knew that she'd prayed about her feelings and her actions, and felt at peace with her decisions.

Now that the decision was made, everything seemed almost easy. The first thing Sam did was speak to Bishop Kropfs.

After discussing things for quite some time, the bishop sat back and stared at him boldly. "Samuel, are you sure about this? You seem to be making these decisions hastily."

"I would agree that to most, these decisions do seem rushed. But I have prayed long and hard about them. And I'm seeking your guidance as well."

"If you leave your life at the college, what are you going to do?"

"I'm hoping to do two things. I'd like to buy some of the land that's adjacent to the family farm and use some of the methods I've been teaching about to increase crop productivity, but I'd also still like to teach some, too."

Bishop Kropfs's brow rose. "Teach who?"

"I'd like to offer farmers in the community some training. And, if you don't mind, I'd like to still teach at the college. Not on a daily basis, but perhaps as a guest lector a few times a year."

"That has a nice ring to it, I'm thinking. And if it's only every now and then, perhaps it won't be too difficult to manage," the bishop added, obviously warming up to the idea. "You could hire a driver, I suppose."

Sam figured relying on other people to get him around might be the hardest adjustment of all. He'd have to learn to depend on others. "I would like to be able to continue teaching. But, I'm also willing to listen to your advice. And, I'm wondering if you all will be able to forgive me for leaving."

"Forgive you for what?"

"For leaving the faith. For trying things out on my own."

"There's no shame in that, Samuel. Everyone has to step out and experience things. We're proud of you. I promise you that. We will discuss this and do some praying, too." He looked up. "I must say I'm surprised. I thought you were happy with how things were."

Sam chose his words carefully. "I was happy.

And, I think I could be happy there for the rest of my life. But lately I've been starting to realize that just having a good career wasn't enough. I need all of me to be fulfilled. Only by marrying in my faith and living my life the way I grew up will give me the sense of peace I've been yearning for."

"We will give it some thought, Samuel."

"*Danke*, Bishop."

After the conversation, Sam went back to the campus to meet with his school's administrator. That discussion was far harder.

"I don't understand, Sam," Bill Ames sputtered. "You've been extremely successful in both the classroom and in the research department."

"I've enjoyed being here a great deal. I don't know if I can explain my feelings other than that I think it's time I went back to my family."

"But aren't they only an hour or two away?"

They were a world apart in other ways. "Yes."

"What are you going to do?" Bill raised an eyebrow. "Do you have plans to go to another university? If so, I feel I have a right—"

"It's not that." Feeling suspiciously like a lad in trouble, Sam figured he had nothing to lose. "Bill, the thing is, there's a woman involved. She's Amish."

"But you are, too. Right?"

"No. We Amish don't join the church until we feel compelled to. I never joined. But I'm ready to join now."

"Couldn't this . . . this woman just come out and live with you?"

"I will not ask her to. Her faith and family are as important to her as breathing."

"But she could. I think you should speak with her."

"I've made my decision. Though, I have asked the Bishop if I could come back as a guest lecturer at times."

"Is that right?"

Sam could feel himself blushing. "I know it's a lot to ask. But I am only following my heart and soul."

"I am starting to realize that. Well, this is going to cause me no small amount of problems. We've already made up the schedule for the fall semester. We've assigned classes to you. Students have signed up."

"I know, and I am sorry about that."

"But not enough to change your mind?"

"No. I'm afraid not."

A dimple appeared in his boss's cheek. "So you're leaving everything for love, huh? When some of the girls hear of this, they're going to swoon."

Sam sat down with a chuckle. "Hopefully, things will work out. I haven't talked to Winnie yet."

"You're taking a leap of faith, then."

"I guess I am," he said with some surprise.

Bill stood up and shook his hand. "I truly do

wish you the best of luck. If you find the opportunity to be a guest lecturer, let me know."

"You'd allow me to do that?"

"Without a doubt. I hope that woman knows how lucky she is. There're not many who would be willing to switch careers and lifestyles like you are."

"If you knew Winnie, you'd know that she'll tell me what she thinks, for better or worse," Sam said as he walked out the door.

To his surprise, he felt lighter and freer than ever.

# Chapter 17

"Have you heard the news?" Katie asked as she entered the *Sitzschtupp*.

"News about what?" Winnie looked up from the wedding ring quilt she was working on. To her dismay, it had taken a broken leg to finally gain the patience needed to complete a project.

"About Samuel Miller, of course. Everyone is saying he's moving back."

Winnie dismissed the gossip with a smile. "That's not news. He's been back for some time, helping Jonathan with the cleanup of the barn and helping Eli with the spring plowing and such." Honestly, sometimes Winnie was sure her sister-in-law loved to make mountains out of molehills.

"It is far more than that, Winnie. He's moving back, for good. He left his college and everything. At least, that's what I heard he talked to the bishop about it." Katie shook her head. "This is surely a season of change. That barn burning has set off a series of events I never would have dreamed."

Startled to find her hands shaking, Winnie pushed the material to one side, not even caring that some of it fell to the floor in a wrinkled heap. "I can't believe Sam would do something like that. He loves his college."

Looking mighty satisfied to have finally gained her sister-in-law's attention, Katie folded her arms over her chest. Somewhat smugly she added, "Perhaps he's found other things to love."

"Nothing you're sayin' is making any sense." Winnie knew her voice was flustered, but she didn't care. "I think we should wait to speak to Sam himself before we go speculating on his future."

"Suit yourself, but I know I'm right. I heard all this straight from Mr. McClusky at the store this morning. He'd heard straight from Lydia Hershberger, who heard from the bishop. It's a fact, Samuel Miller is coming back."

"My word."

Katie rushed over and hugged her tight. "Oh, Winnie, I'm so happy for you."

"Stop talking like that, wouldja?" She was too nervous for so much teasing!

"Surely you don't have to be so cross."

"I'm not trying to be bad-tempered. I just don't want to hear any more talk and gossip about Samuel."

"Do you want me to leave, then?" came a voice from the doorway.

Winnie whipped her head toward Sam—toward that voice she'd know anywhere. "I didn't know you were here."

"Jonathan let me in." With a gentle smile, he stepped closer. "So, may I come in, or would you rather I leave you alone?"

Katie beamed. "Of course, Samuel. Come sit down."

Winnie just stared. She felt helpless and out of control, like she was stuck in the center of a tornado. Gingerly, she got to her feet, anxious to at least be able to face him that way. "How much did you hear?"

"Enough."

"You shouldn't have listened."

"I couldn't help it. Your conversation was pretty important. I sure didn't want to interrupt."

"Still—"

Katie cleared her throat meaningfully. "Honestly, Winnie. What is wrong with you?"

"Nothing." It was just she was terribly embarrassed.

Samuel came closer, now standing mere feet away from her. "I was hoping we could have a conversation—not an argument."

"Yes. I . . . I've been wanting to talk to you, too." However, inside, she felt as if everything was off kilter.

"You could talk now," Katie said, all smiles.

"I'd like to talk. Privately." Winnie sent a meaningful glare Katie's way.

Katie finally caught the hint. "I think I'll go upstairs. I'll take the girls, too."

"Thank you."

Sam's gaze turned guarded. "Winnie? What is going on with you?"

"Not as much as with you, I'm coming to find out," Winnie replied, feeling somewhat shaken up inside. Her heart seemed to be beating double time.

"What is that supposed to mean?"

"It means that I've just discovered that you intend to stay here. That you intend to join the church."

Samuel took a chair. "Please, Win, let's sit down and talk things over." When she did as he asked, he surprised her once again by reaching for her hand. "Here's what I've been thinking. I thought maybe that way we could maybe try courting a bit. I met with the bishop and I think I've got everything arranged."

"To do what? Quit your job?"

"Well, yes."

The tears fell, and she didn't even try to hide them. "But why?"

"Because I can't be all things to everyone. I chose you."

"Really?"

He squeezed her hand. "Yes, really. What are you upset about?"

"Sam, I've been wantin' to talk to you, too. To tell you that I would leave the order for you to be happy. I've been praying about it, and I think I would make a mighty fine professor's wife. If . . . if we came to that."

He stood frozen. "You would have done that?"

"Yes, if that's what would have made you happy."

"But, Winnie, I never even considered asking you to do such a thing. The outside world is so different."

"Maybe. Maybe not. We would have each other, and you would be happy. That was going to be good enough for me." Glaring at him, she chided, "Unfortunately, you didn't even think to talk to me about it. You didn't care enough to seek my opinion."

"But you have it wrong, Winnie. It wasn't that I didn't trust you. Or that I didn't care about you. See—I wanted to surprise you."

"You certainly did that." She wanted to unbend, but she still felt a bit foolish—and dismayed. Perhaps they should take things more slowly?

"Winnie Lundy, I'm not giving up on us. I aim to court you."

Looking at their hands, at their fingers linked together, Winnie knew she'd never felt more breathless. Never felt so happy. Never felt so confused. Slowly, she looked up at him. "Why?"

"Because I can't help myself," he said simply. "Whenever I think of my future, I now imagine you in it. And here is the place for us. This community. Among the Amish."

"You wouldn't miss your university?"

"Not as much as I would miss you." He almost smiled.

So did she. Perhaps their foolishness was over. Now that all their obstacles were being removed, they would finally be able to concentrate on just the two of them, and how they felt about each other. "I would miss you, too, if you went back to the English."

Then it seemed only natural for her to reach for his other hand. It felt only right to link her fingers through that hand, too.

To simply just appreciate how much Sam had come to mean to her.

"So, may I call on you again soon?"

"Yes. As long as you announce yourself instead of lurking around doorways."

He tapped his head. "I'll try and remember that."

And then he was gone. Giggling like a schoolgirl, Winnie fell back on the couch. For the first time in a long while, she felt pretty and fresh. Wanted. It was a right *gut* feeling, indeed.

# Chapter 18

David couldn't catch his breath. His chest hurt something fierce and his lungs burned, like a pile of hot coals were sitting on his chest, weighing him down, preventing him from moving.

The worst had happened. Jonathan Lundy had found out the truth.

Just a few moments earlier, Jonathan had shown up by his side at the lake and boldly stated that he knew David was the one.

The person who'd set fire to his barn.

And now all the air inside of him seemed to have left.

"David, surely you're not going to pretend you didn't hear me. Don't you have anything to say?"

"Ah . . . yes." In the space of two heartbeats, David slowly managed to meet his gaze. Those crystal blue eyes that had always seemed so patient and sad, especially after the first Mrs. Lundy had died, looked nothing like they usually did. Instead, the man's pupils looked like ice, like the depths of the skating pond come March, when the top layer was so thin you could see underneath it.

He gathered himself together. Looking back down at his boots, so scuffed, on account they'd been his older brother's, he murmured, "There's nothin' to say." He winced, automatically flinched when he heard his words out loud. This was about the time his pa would have backhanded him for speaking at all.

But instead of looking even more angry, Jonathan sighed. "So it's gonna be like this, is it?"

"Like what?"

"Like you pretendin' you don't know what I'm talking about and like me pretending I'm not hurt." Looking across at the stillness of the pond, he shook his head sadly. "To tell you the truth, I'd kinda hoped things would be different."

David had hoped his secret would stay hidden forever. That he'd never be having this conversation. But it was finally time to face his punishment. "There's nothin' to talk about. I burnt your barn and never told no one."

Around them, clouds filled the sky. Within the hour, rain would come, treating the tiny seedlings in the fields beyond to a much needed drink of water. Cooling things off for a bit.

"I suppose that's how things could be described." Turning away from the water, Jonathan faced David again. "Is that how things happened exactly? All of a sudden, you got a bee in your bonnet to harm my family?"

David couldn't help it—he flinched. But he didn't try to defend himself. There was no defense.

Jonathan's eyes narrowed. "Well? You want me to be guessin' again? All right. So, you reckoned you wanted to kill my horses?"

David bit his lip to keep from talking.

"You wanted to go to jail?" An eyebrow raised. "You wanted to hurt Winnie?" He leaned forward just as David tasted the sharp metallic hint of blood. "Is that it? For some reason, you're upset with my family? Is that what happened?"

"No . . . I . . ." How could he answer those questions? He felt so helpless. What excuse could he possibly give?

"All right, then. I suppose we have the answer." Roughly, Jonathan grabbed him by the collar. "Come with me. We'll go down to the sheriff's office and I'll press charges. You tried to murder me and my family when we haven't done anything."

"No!"

Miraculously, Jonathan's iron grip eased. "No? Then what happened? How did that fire come to be? Talk, boy," he whispered. "You've got nothing to lose and only the truth to gain."

"The fire was an accident." Tears started to fall. His voice cracked. He struggled to breathe as everything that he'd tried so hard to hold in threatened to fall, to break apart, to burst through him. "I promise, I never meant for it to happen, I never meant to harm the horses."

"Ah."

But now that he'd set his tongue in motion, it appeared in no great hurry to stop. The words rushed out. "Please believe me—I would never mean to hurt Winnie. Or you. I didn't mean to. I was tryin' . . ." He struggled to talk. "I was trying to . . ." He couldn't say it.

Jonathan pushed. "Trying to what?"

To David's surprise, Jonathan reached out and took hold of his hand. As if he felt David's scars, he gently turned his palm over and examined the rough, angry skin that was taking so very long to heal. Clicking his tongue he said, "I don't know if it makes things any easier, but the Lord already knows the truth."

"If He knows, He doesn't care. I asked Him to make everything better. He didn't."

"Our Lord can't verra well go putting burnt barns back together, can he?"

"I asked him to guide me to know what to do. To help me. He didn't."

"He guided you here, to this conversation. That counts for something, I'm thinkin'."

"But He grants miracles in the Bible."

"David, it's my belief that some miracles are small. The love of a family member. The beauty of a sun-filled day. See, He grants us miracles even when we don't deserve them." Jonathan released his hand and crouched in front of David just as the rain started to fall all around them. "Jesus already knows our sins but loves us anyway. He already knows our sufferings, our weaknesses, our dreams, and he loves us anyway," he said again. "Always. No matter what."

"You really believe that?"

"With all my heart. There's some good in that, don'tcha think?"

David had never thought of the Lord already knowing things. In a way, it did make him feel better. To not have to hold secrets anymore.

But why, then, hadn't he already gotten in trouble? "Why hasn't God punished me?"

Jonathan looked him over. "Maybe He already has. You look like you've been carrying a heavy burden all on your own. Perhaps it's time to share some of that weight. Please talk to me, David. If you didn't mean my family harm, tell me what happened that night. I need to know. And, I have a feeling, you might need to share the story."

Whether it was Jonathan's words, or the way the man's hand was curved protectively around his own, or the light cleansing rain falling from the sky, David finally felt able to talk. "I should first tell you that I don't have too many friends. I don't know why." When the older man said nothing, only nodded, David continued.

"Sometime back, some boys had gotten hold of cigarettes and were selling them. I took some money that I'd saved and bought a few packs and two lighters. For the first time, the other boys looked at me like I fit in."

"And so you started smoking?"

"*Jah*. At first, I was no good, but then I got better. When a few others started talkin' about some *Englischers* who could make smoke rings, and they talked like they admired that, I decided to try and make them, too."

Instead of glaring, Jonathan merely looked reflective. "I imagine those would be difficult to make."

"I got pretty good at it. But I wanted to be real good, so next time I saw everyone I could show them." Oh, his pride and vanity had cost so much.

"And did you?"

David shook his head. "No. That night, I went to your barn. It's not too far from our house, you know. Plus, the loft doesn't have any windows. No one would see the sparks of the cigarettes in the night."

"And so there you were."

"Yes. I was tryin' to make smoke rings. I could just make out their forms in the dim light peering up from the windows below. I was trying so hard, I hadn't put out one of the old cigarettes so well." He swallowed. The sparks, the memories, were as vivid as if they'd happened hours instead of weeks before. "When the hay caught on fire, there wasn't anything I could do. I tried to stop it. There was a horse blanket, I tried to smother the flames, but they just seemed to eat up the fabric instead of be hindered by it."

"And you burned your hands."

David looked at his palms. "I did. By then, there were flames everywhere. It was too late." Daring to look at Jonathan, David murmured, "I promise,

I tried to put out the flames, but it all happened so fast."

"I know."

"At first I was going to wake you up, but I heard you yelling. And then I didn't know what to do. I was too afraid to come out of the shadows. So . . . I ran."

With a heavy sigh, Jonathan stood up. "It's a blessing you weren't hurt. Things would have been verra bad indeed if you hadn't gotten out in time. Oh, David. What would have happened if you had died in the fire?"

David had never thought of that. It had never even occurred to him to think about what would have happened if he had really gotten hurt.

It had never occurred to him to be grateful for anything.

Surely the Lord hadn't spared him for a reason. But, the Lord never did things without a purpose. Did He?

Continuing the story, he murmured, "I jumped from the loft just as the flames spread and your horses started screaming. I meant to go get them, but then I heard you coming and . . . and I was scared." As two tears slid down his cheeks, he whispered, "I was so afraid."

"I would have been afraid, too," Jonathan said softly. After a moment, he said, "And then, you went home?"

"I did. When I got there, my *daed* was already

getting ready to go to your place. I knew he'd never forgive me if he knew what I'd done. If he knew I'd been careless and a coward. If he'd known that I'd run. So . . . so I hid. When he left, and the house was quiet, I washed up the best I could, got into bed and pretended to sleep."

"Only pretended?"

"All I could hear in my head was the roar of the fire and the horses screaming." Lowering his voice, he confessed, "When I closed my eyes all I could hear were my faults. That's still all I hear."

With a weary expression, Jonathan nodded. "Now I know the truth."

David wiped his cheeks and tried to prepare himself for what had to come next. They had to tell his father. Next, of course, would be to tell the authorities.

His voice husky, Jonathan asked, "Have you prayed for forgiveness?"

The question surprised him. "No."

"Maybe it's time you did."

"I . . . I will."

Jonathan gazed at him again, his eyes almost looking regretful. "I think you'll feel better for that."

Perhaps it was Jonathan's own sad expression that gave him strength—perhaps it was hearing that God already knew what he'd done. But from somewhere deep inside, David finally found the strength to do what he'd wanted to from the moment the first piece of hay ignited.

Closing his eyes, he spoke from his heart. "I am sorry, Jonathan. I will do whatever I can to help make things right."

After saying the words, David found he could breathe again. The horrible burden that had been suffocating him seemed to have lifted. With that weight lifting, he felt almost normal. He opened his eyes. The world around him was still the same, but it seemed brighter. He felt stronger, too. He'd done it. He'd followed the Lord's will, he'd faced the worst, and was prepared to accept the consequences.

Jonathan sighed. Then, to David's surprise, he stepped forward. Holding out his hand, he gently shook David's. "I accept your apology."

And then he turned and walked away. Around them, the fine droplets created a kind of hazy mist, blurring their surroundings. The haziness seemed to fit the moment—it blurred everything, which was how David was feeling.

What was going on? Surely after everything that had occurred, Jonathan wasn't just gonna leave? After a slight pause, David rushed after him. "Jonathan, *Mr. Lundy*. Wait. Please."

He stopped. "Yes?"

"What are you gonna do now?"

Still without turning, Jonathan replied, "I need to get back to work."

"I mean . . . I mean about me."

Slowly, he faced David again. "I expect you might help out with the barn raising. There's a lot to do and I'll need every able man."

"But—"

"Don't even think of getting out of it. Even men with hurt hands can contribute. I expect to see you with your family."

"But what about the authorities?" he sputtered. "What about my father? Aren't you going to tell on me? Don't you want me to be punished?"

"To be honest, for days and weeks, I have sought vengeance. I wanted someone to blame. I wanted to be able to understand why such a thing would happen to *me*." He rubbed a hand along his beard. "See, I was only thinking of myself, I'm afraid. You know I lost a wife. I thought surely that was enough pain for a man to bear. The fire was terribly hard for me to understand."

"I see."

Jonathan shook his head. "No, I don't know if you do. I didn't want to forgive, but after hearing your story, I realized I have been wrong. See, sometimes, accidents happen." Looking out beyond David, he murmured, "Fear and pride can take over in a heartbeat. It can make even the best of us do terrible things. Making you hurt more will not make me feel better."

"But I did a terrible thing."

"David, what happened *was* terrible. But you

didn't do it on purpose. It was an accident. You've apologized to me. That is enough."

"But my father—"

"You've discussed things with the only Father I care about. He is the one who guides my life. He is the one I have to answer to. Because of that, I am satisfied."

Jonathan stepped away, then, after turning and spying David standing there, did something truly amazing, he stepped closer and pulled David into a hug. "You will be all right, David. The next time we see each other, all will be good. I promise you that."

David could only nod as tears slid down his cheeks, mixing with the mist. Sometime during their conversation, he, too, began to realize that there was only one Father in his life as well. That although his own family situation wasn't as he'd hoped, he could bear it, because it was only a temporary circumstance. Soon he would be a man with his own family.

And one day he'd be in the eternal kingdom, and that would be the nicest place of all.

# Chapter 19

Instead of going back to the house or to work, Jonathan took a detour and drove his buggy along some of the small, windy roads that had connected various plots of land with each other—and had for generations.

The crisp air held a touch of warmth behind it, reminding him that time, as always, moved on, no matter what the circumstances.

That thought had never felt more true. His conversation with David had been revealing, indeed. But, if he were honest, it was also God's whispers in his ear that had been the most telling. During that hour, Jonathan had never felt closer to the Lord, never more open to His will.

Lost in thought, he slowed Blacky's pace. When the horse restlessly bobbed his head, Jonathan parked the buggy to the side, near a thicket of fresh spring grass that the horse could easily munch on if desired.

Then he got out of the buggy and walked a ways up. Scanning the horizon, he could just see the faint outline of the Brenneman Bed and Breakfast. To the other side, he could see the shadows of the Hostetler barn.

Jonathan knew the family well—it was impossible not to know all the surrounding families well, their community was so tightly knit. And while his had never been a perfect life, Jonathan had always known that the Hostetlers' circumstances were difficult, indeed.

They were not well liked.

Oh, Jonathan figured he could have tried harder to reach out to them. They all could have tried harder. But Amos Hostetler was a somewhat difficult man, without humor. His wife was cowed and meek to the point where it was difficult to have even the most simple of conversations. Their children—all eight of them—were good enough, but a little standoffish. Jonathan's Mary had put it best—they weren't good playmates.

Rumors had circulated that perhaps Amos was too hard on the children. Some blamed his farm's continual financial problems for Amos's short temper.

Jonathan had a feeling that Amos was just that way.

And empathizing with David—hearing the admission in his voice, seeing the fear and resignation as he told his tale—was like a blow to his belly. Jonathan felt that nothing positive would be accomplished by involving David's father.

When the Lord had guided him, whispered in his ear, Jonathan had suddenly known what to do.

It was time to forgive.

He'd been so caught up in his anger, so determined to seek justice, that he'd neglected to realize that there were other feelings and viewpoints involved.

Seeking retribution from David and his family would not bring his barn back. It would not erase the all-encompassing fear that had engulfed him when he'd worried about Winnie.

When he'd been afraid for his animals' lives.

The memories would still be there. And perhaps that is what needed to be. Those memories were strong. Not only of the bad things, but of the good things, too. Of how all their neighbors pulled together and offered support.

Of how his boss Brent was offering to give him the wood for the barn, and offered to shut down the mill for a half day so everyone could help. That was a gift greater than he could have imagined.

So was the gleam of hope in David's eyes. Jonathan had no doubt the boy would help build the barn as much as he could. He also knew that the guilt and weight of his actions would be with him forever.

But perhaps the memories of Jonathan's forgiveness would be there as well. And perhaps that forgiveness would ignite a new flame in his heart and lead David to be the man he wanted to become, instead of the one he thought he had to be.

Winnie looked, then looked again when she saw who was driving up the long, winding road to their farm. The buggy was definitely Eli's, but the form in the front seat certainly was not the lanky body of Eli Miller.

Who could it be?

She was even more curious when the buggy horse sidestepped a bit near a patch of bushes. Something had spooked it, and the driver was having a difficult time finding his bearings.

Or so it seemed.

"Who's that?" Hannah asked as she came to stand beside Winnie at the front window.

"I'm not sure." As she'd done more times than she could count, Winnie picked Hannah up and sat her on the kitchen counter. "Someone's comin' in Eli Miller's buggy, but I don't think it's him."

Hannah scrambled to her knees as she peered out. "*Jah*. It don't look like Eli."

Mary joined them. "Isn't that a courtin' buggy? Eli doesn't drive that around, does he?"

"Not for some time." Glancing at her niece in some surprise, Winnie said, "I'm surprised you knew about courtin' buggies."

"I like them. They're prettier, don'tcha think?"

"I do." Winnie always enjoyed riding in the fancier, sleeker buggy with its open top. It was far more enjoyable than the sedate, closed-in buggy. Staring at the driver again, she murmured, "Could that be Caleb?"

Little Hannah clapped. "Oh, I hope so! I like Caleb."

"That man's not Caleb," Mary stated without a

bit of doubt in her voice as the buggy approached. She squinted and pressed her nose to the window-pane, creating a smudge that would need to be washed off with vinegar. "It looks to be Samuel."

As the buggy stopped and the driver alighted, Hannah held out her arms for Winnie to help her down. After Winnie complied, she ran to the door and scampered down the front steps before Winnie could say a word. "Samuel!" she cried, loud enough to startle all the animals in the barn.

In a moment's time, Mary joined her sister.

Sam greeted both girls with friendly hugs, then helped them climb up to the bench of the buggy; they so obviously wanted to try out the seat.

This time it was Winnie who wanted to press her nose to the pane and watch more closely, because she certainly did not want to miss a moment of what was happening.

If she wasn't mistaken, Samuel Miller was dressed Amish and had just arrived in a courting buggy. "What in the world?" she murmured. Stranger things had happened, but not for some time.

When the girls got off the buggy, Mary turned to the window. "Winnie! Winnie, come out, why don'tcha?"

Winnie knew her cheeks were likely blazing red. She was mighty thankful neither Jonathan nor Katie were around to comment about that. But still, she waited.

"Winnie? Winnie!" Hannah sung out. "Come on!"

Well, it looked to be out of her hands now. "I'm on my way," Winnie murmured, though she knew no one could hear her. Carefully, she made her way through the kitchen and did her best to meet them, glad that she hardly needed help anymore.

In a flash, Sam was up the steps, stepping behind her and gently closing the door. She could hardly do a thing besides stare at him.

He seemed to be enjoying every bit of her surprise. "Hi."

*"Gut-n-owed,"* she said formally.

Hat in hand, Sam looked amused. "Good afternoon, to you, too."

Darting a look at Mary and Hannah, she was pleased to see they were off playing with their dog near the garden. Since this was one of their favorite activities, she wasn't worried about them. Not near as worried about them as she was about her beating heart!

The only thing to do was to offer Samuel something to drink. "Would you care for some lemonade?"

"I would." Already walking to the kitchen door, he motioned for her to sit on one of the many chairs decorating the front porch. "I'll get it."

She sat. Not because she needed the rest for her foot, but because she couldn't believe what was happening.

In no time at all, he was back with two glasses in his hands. After passing her one, he sat down next to her. "This drink is a blessing. It sure is hot."

"It is most pleasant—" Oh, she couldn't do this. "Why are you dressed Amish?" she blurted. "Why did you arrive in a buggy? In a courtin' buggy, of all things? What is going on?"

"It's like I told you the other day. I'm going to join the church."

"Yes, but I didn't think you would do it so suddenly. Where's your truck? Your Ford?" She'd liked his shiny black truck. She'd always thought he looked right fittin' in that bold vehicle.

"I sold it."

Lemonade sputtered everywhere. "Samuel Miller, you start talking this minute. When do you plan to be baptised?"

"On Sunday."

"Are you sure you don't need more time to consider things?"

"I'm positive." Then, sheepishly, he grinned as he lifted one leg. "Well, I might need more time to get some proper clothes. The pants are Eli's and they're mighty short."

Turning serious, he said, "Winnie, now that my decision has been made, I'm anxious to return to the community. I've missed my family. I've missed our community and the strength and comfort it gave me. And, then, there was a certain mouthy dark-haired woman with the prettiest dimples I ever saw. I've started thinking about her quite a bit."

Winnie couldn't believe her ears. This was really happening. All the feelings she'd been trying to stifle unsuccessfully could now be brought to light. She could begin to hope again.

"I still hate to think of you giving up everything."

"I'm ready. When I was younger, it felt as if my brain was too big for my head. All I wanted to do was learn and learn and ask questions. I was never more sure in my life when I asked my family to let me go study. I needed to learn as much as I needed to breathe."

"And then?"

"I followed where I thought the Lord was guiding me. I was sure there was a reason he made me so smart. I felt it would be wrong not to see where it all led me." After a sip of lemonade, he continued. "I loved going to university. I loved the challenge. But, Winnie, there's more to me than this brain of mine. And, there's more in my head than just a desire for knowledge. I want family and love and my faith."

"I know you love your family. I've never doubted that. I don't think anyone has."

Looking almost boyish, Sam tilted his head. "Oh, but you're going to make me say this, aren't ya? All right, I will. I care for you, Winnie."

For once, Winnie couldn't think of a single

response. Her lungs felt out of breath, like she was struggling for air. For so long, she'd longed to be loved. To have someone in her life who cared about her . . . and who she cared deeply about.

For some time now, she knew that person was Sam. But she didn't want her love to cause him regrets. She didn't want him one day wishing he'd never left his English world.

Sam's hazel eyes glinted. "Don't make us wait, Winnie." He leaned forward, bracing his elbows on his knees. "Don't make me wait another day for you to be my girl."

The childish expression made her smile. After all, they were two adults in their twenties. Hardly star-crossed teens.

Yet, being his "girl" sounded awfully right. But still, scary.

"I . . . I don't know." Truly, she was still trying to get her head around the fact that everything she'd hoped for was coming true.

"Do you want to take things slow? We can do that, if you'd like."

"I would like slow, if you don't mind."

"I don't mind at all. You are worth it. And the life I want with you is worth it, too."

Oh, so was he. After all the past disappointments in love, Winnie now knew it had been the Lord's way of preparing her for this relationship—the relationship with Samuel that she could rely on for the rest of her life.

She'd needed those trials and tribulations to be strong enough to start a life with Samuel. She needed past experiences so that she'd be wise enough to understand Sam's feelings when he talked about his past. He stood up. "So, Winnie Lundy, would you care to go for a ride in my borrowed courting buggy?"

Winnie couldn't help it, she laughed. "I'd love to, but I'm not certain you need an extra passenger just yet."

With a grimace, he said, "I forgot horses have minds of their own."

"I'm just teasing you. You'll get the hang of things again soon. But I'm sorry, I canna go. I'm watching the girls for Katie today. She's over with Anna, helping with some wedding things."

He finished his lemonade, sat it on the wide planks of the porch, then stood up. "Maybe tomorrow? In the afternoon?"

"I'm working until four o'clock. If you come over after dinner, I'd love to go for a ride."

Almost shyly, Samuel Miller smiled. "Then I'll be back."

Winnie could only nod as he stepped down the stairs. He waved goodbye to the girls, and then coaxed Eli's horse on his way again.

If that don't beat all. She had a beau. A fine man, too. Samuel Miller.

# Chapter 20

From the porch, Winnie felt a great sense of satisfaction and excitement as she watched the men bond together in work teams and the women carry overstuffed baskets toward the shade of the oak and walnut trees.

Today was a special day, indeed. With God's help—and everyone else's—by nightfall they'd have the makings of a new barn.

"Well, those men are certainly as busy as can be. We best not stand here too much longer. We'll be sproutin' feathers when we have important work to do," Irene Brenneman said. "We need to plan where all the ladies are going to put their dishes."

Winnie pointed to the dining room, where the long oak table was covered with an assortment of quilts. Since Katie was busy trying to tend to everyone, Winnie was doing her best to plan the logistics. "I'll direct the ladies and the food here on the table. They can leave their baskets with quilts and dishes near the trees." As two children skipped rope nearby, Winnie winced, just imagining how difficult it would be to stay organized with so many children underfoot. "And, I think we should encourage the *kinner* to go play on the other side of the house near the garden."

As the hours passed, Winnie noticed the men falling into place, each doing what they did best.

Jonathan instructed groups, John Brenneman double-checked supplies, and Brent, Jonathan's boss at the lumberyard, explained how he organized the lumber. Finally, with much good humor and teasing about who was the strongest, the barn raising began.

Voices and music rang out, children scampered and laughed in the vibrant green fields, and the scents of hearty food and sawdust filled the air.

For all the hard work, it was great fun.

All the while, Winnie did her best to stay near the construction, all in hopes of catching a glimpse of Samuel.

She wasn't disappointed. Whether by design or chance, she saw quite a bit of him throughout the morning. His smiles and nods in her direction were worth all the knowing looks and teasing glances from the other women.

Finally lunch was served. After a quick, silent moment of prayer, Winnie took her place at Sam's table and brought over plates of chicken and bowls of potatoes.

*"Danke,"* he said, when she brought him a festive-looking gelatin salad.

"You're welcome," she murmured with a smile. Even though she'd done no part of the meal except to serve it.

It was customary for the women and children to eat after the men had their chance. When Winnie took Sam's spot, she hardly noticed what she put in her mouth—all she could think about was how handsome he'd been. How the same yet different he seemed around the other men.

How smitten she was with him. A warmth filled her. Could this really be her future, a life working side by side with such a generous, giving, handsome man? It all seemed too good to be true.

"Winnie, if you're not too tired, we've got a good amount of work to do, if you're done sittin'," Irene called.

"I'm not tired, my leg feels fine." She hopped up. "I'll be right there."

Just as the sun set, a shadow fell across the front porch. The barn frame was up. Families began to take their leave, gathering sleepy children and sparkly clean food containers.

Jonathan, Katie, and the girls were inside getting the girls ready for bed.

Winnie sat on the front stoop in the shadow of the new structure and breathed a sigh of contentment. The day had been a busy one, but most gratifying. Barn raisings were always a pure example of their way of life. She was never so proud to be Amish. Once more, she knew she'd be counting her blessings for many days to come.

She was just about to do that when yet another shadow fell over her—this one far smaller. Ah, yet another blessing, indeed. "Samuel. I thought you had already left."

"Without telling you goodbye? I wouldn't do that."

"The barn, it looks *gut, jah*?"

His tawny brown hair was still damp from when he washed up. As was his habit, he brushed it out of his face and looked at the structure. "It's a fine building. I don't think I'll ever be able to look at it without remembering this feeling of accomplishment. I'm pleased with it."

"You should. It's a right beautiful barn. My brother is so pleased."

Sam smiled as he dropped down to sit next to her. "Have I told you today how glad I am to see you're back on two feet?" Sam said, his eyes twinkling in the way that made her heart melt.

"Not half as glad as I am. I was thinking those crutches would always be my companions." Carefully, shaking her right leg, she said, "Though I have some scars, I feel like I did before the fire."

"The scars are a small price to pay for being healthy again, I think." Pointing to the new barn, he said, "This building kind of feels like my life right now. Though the old structure has gone away, the memories will always be there."

"And in its place?"

"In its place is something new and fresh. Supported by many strong hands and hearts."

"That's a fitting description, I think. Samuel, I am mighty glad you decided to come back. I would have become English for you, but I don't know if

I'd have ever fit in the way you would've needed me to."

"I think you would have done all right, but I'm glad I'm the one who did the changing."

"You don't think you'll have regrets?"

"No. Especially since the bishop felt I could still teach at the college a bit." Flashing a smile, he added, "Like the fire in the barn, what happened was unexpected, but now that time has passed, I see that it was not all bad."

He held out his hand for her to take. "With the Lord's help, I think we'll see in the coming years that it will prove to be the right thing."

She placed her other hand over their joined ones and squeezed gently. Oh, she never wanted to let him go! "I know what we have is the right thing, indeed."

"May I come by tomorrow?"

"I'd be terribly sad if you didn't."

"That's it? No exceptions or rules or circumstances?"

"Like you, I feel new again. Being hurt in the fire taught me to count my blessings more. I'm going to count you as my greatest blessing."

Slowly, Sam lifted her hands and gently kissed her knuckles. Winnie didn't even try to pretend that she didn't feel a rush of pleasure from his touch.

She would never have dreamed that she'd spend a full week in a hospital with burns and a broken foot. And even more, that it would all lead to finally thinking of marriage.

Funny how so much of what she used to worry about didn't bother her anymore.

"You know, one day, we might look back at all this and laugh."

Still looking at their joined hands, Sam said, "About how we met?"

"About how the Lord really does have a plan. And that His plan is both wondrous and true."

"And never ceases to amaze."

Winnie looked up at him and smiled. "I've fallen in love with you."

"And I you." Slowly, Samuel Miller leaned close and gently brushed his lips against hers, and then kissed Winnie again.

Right there, on the front stoop of her brother's home. In the shadow of a freshly built barn, where all things seemed possible.

# *Epilogue*

"*Gude Mariye,* Anna!" Katie called out from the doorway. "It's time to wake up, and to be quick about it, too! I canna believe you are sleeping so late on your own wedding day."

"Late?" Anna peeked out of the covers, then groaned. "It's barely light out. What time is it?"

"Five. Come now, there's much to be done." Looking a bit shamefaced, Katie said, "I know it's early, but I'm fair to bursting with excitement."

As usual, Katie's enthusiasm was contagious. Sitting up, Anna looked fondly at the woman who had once, long ago, been just a good friend. Now she was about to be her sister.

*Henry!*

"Have you seen your brother yet?"

A sweet, knowing smile filled Katie's gaze. "I have."

"How's he doing? Is he *neahfich*?" Oh, she really hoped he wasn't. If he was apprehensive, perhaps that meant he really regretted everything. Or was having second thoughts?

"He looks nervous, indeed."

"He does?"

Katie broke into a broad grin. "But not for the reason you're thinkin'—it's because he hopes everything will go okay."

"Oh. Well, I, myself feel extremely happy! I'm finally getting married."

"I'll be happy when you get out of bed. It's time for breakfast. People will be arriving in just a few hours and we've much to do before that. There's a bit of baking that still needs to be done."

The ceremony was supposed to begin at eight that morning. During the ceremony, they'd sing hymnals from the *Ausbund*, have scripture readings, and read passages from the *Ordnung*. They wouldn't be fully good and married until noon. After that would be a wonderful chicken dinner and pies.

She pushed the covers away and stepped out of bed. "All right. I'll get busy. I better get my parents up. It will probably take them the whole time to get ready."

"You're wrong," Katie said with a smile. "Your *mamm* beat me up! She's helping my *mamm* and Rebecca sort through the plates and such from the wedding wagon."

Anna knew she shouldn't be so shocked. Anna had forgotten but was reminded, time and again over the last year, of the many good qualities her mother had in abundance. She was earnest, had a desire to please, and above all, she had an infinite love for Anna. And Anna loved her, too.

Though she wasn't quite the baker Irene was, she could certainly make fine pies and other baked goods. She also had a knack for planning large events—whether they were English or Amish. With Irene's blessing, she helped organize tables and count linens—no small task for a guest list of over two hundred people.

"I'm glad she came," Anna said. "I should go visit with her."

"That's a *gut* idea, I think," Katie murmured.

Anna's bridal gown was a new dress of light blue. Though without adornment, it looked special to her eyes—perhaps because the brand-new dress symbolized so much. Now, though, she ran downstairs in yesterday's dress, a plain gray one which she'd been taken to wearing when work or chores would be especially consuming.

The group in the kitchen looked up in surprise when she appeared. "Up already?"

"Katie made sure of it."

Irene chuckled. "How about some breakfast?"

"Thank you." Though her stomach was in knots, Anna knew it would be wise to eat a hearty meal. The rest of the day would be spent visiting with the great number of people who had traveled to spend the special day with her.

After Irene prepared a plate of fruit, eggs, and toast, Anna's mom brought it to her. "Here you go, honey."

Anna patted the seat of the chair next to her. "Will you sit with me, Mom?"

"Of course." A pretty, familiar smile she loved

passed over her mother's expression. "How are you doing?"

"I'm excited."

"I'm glad. It's a special day. Henry is a good man. You chose well, Anna."

Anna knew that had cost her a lot to say. When Anna had first fallen in love with Henry, her mother—rightfully—had doubted her motivations. But during the past year, it had been her mother who had made all the changes. Now here she was, helping in the kitchen to prepare a feast that was most likely very different than the wedding and reception she'd dreamed of hosting for her daughter. "Have I told you lately that I'm glad you're my mom? You've been a wonderful mother to me."

Her mother blinked. "You've forgiven me for not trusting you to know what's best?"

Anna nodded. "I shouldn't have held a grudge. I'm sorry it's taken me so long to accept your apology."

Her mom wiped her eyes. "I'm proud of you. You've made a wonderful life here for yourself."

A wave of relief and happiness passed over Anna. Finally, it seemed as if everything was right in the world. In her world, the only place that mattered that morning.

After breakfast, all the women got busy making casseroles and baking two more pies. Anna was happy to see that her mother didn't mind in the least doing so much work. In fact, she looked to be enjoying the cheery banter of all the women surrounding them.

Two hours later, from the corner of the kitchen, Katie cleared her throat. "Anna, I can't hold my tongue a moment longer. You must go get ready! The ceremony will start before we know it."

Her mother stood up and held out a hand. "I'd like to help, if I could."

Grasping it, Anna smiled. "I'd love your help. Thank you."

Henry and Anna's wedding ceremony was wonderful-*gut*, Winnie thought. She liked seeing all the English there, at first looking a bit awkward, then settling in and enjoying the ceremony with as much care and sentiment as everyone else.

Winnie had always thought there was something magical about hearing and seeing the old rituals come to life and remembering vows spoken before.

Across the aisle with all the men sat Sam. He was sitting next to Eli and Caleb. If she hadn't been looking for his muscular form, she might have had to look a bit harder, he blended in so well. Now it felt as if all their pasts hardly mattered. Only the present and their future goals were what counted.

Right before she was set to join the other women as they prepared all the food, Sam caught her. "Got a minute?"

Winnie knew she'd spare him any amount of time. "Sure."

"The wedding was a good one, don'tcha think?"

"I do."

"It got me thinking . . ." His words floated away as a group of neighbors nodded in their direction before moving off.

When they were alone again, Winnie said, "What got you thinking?"

"I'm hoping we'll be as happy one day, too. I mean, I would be happy if you"—he stopped, obviously looking impatient with himself—"oh, Winnie, I'm not doing a good job of this am I?"

"I'm not sure. It depends what you're trying to do."

"I know we've been courting a bit, and that you wanted to take things slow, but well, I'd like you to marry me soon. If you would like."

Well, there it was. Her proposal from Samuel. It had happened. Just like that!

The words were much like she expected but the moment was like nothing she'd ever imagined. She felt giddy and pleased . . . and at peace.

Winnie felt right. "Well, now, I think you're doing just fine."

"Then, what do you say?" Samuel looked her over, his beautiful hazel eyes brimming with emotion. "Do you have an answer?"

Reaching out for him, Winnie took his hand. "Oh, Samuel. For such a smart man, you can sure be *deerich,* so foolish! Of course it's a yes. It's always been a yes for you. Always."

If they'd been alone, Winnie guessed they might have kissed. Instead, surrounded by so many who loved and cared for them, he just smiled.

Across the lawn, she caught Katie's eye. When Katie raised her brows in question, Winnie nodded.

Then, when Katie let out a little squeal, Anna looked up. After sharing a glance with Katie, Anna turned to Winnie and grinned.

Yes, it was a special day for all of them. A day to remember and hold close to their hearts for a long time to come. A day for brides and engagements . . . and futures to plan.

And oh, what wonderful things were surely in store!

Giving in to temptation, Winnie spun in a circle and laughed. What wonderful things, indeed.

Dear Reader,

Thank you so much for picking up *Forgiven*. I hope you enjoyed Winnie and Sam's story. What a journey this Sisters of the Heart series has been! I've so enjoyed the Brenneman family and writing about Anna's journey to finding love and acceptance. Now that I've come to the end of the series, I'm sad to see them go.

As always, I have many people to thank. The top of the list is Clara, whose humor and genuine kindness have influenced me greatly. Thank you, as well, to the American Christian Fiction Writers. Joining their ranks has been very rewarding. I know I will also be eternally grateful to the many readers who have taken time to write me notes. Their encouragement always brightens my day.

I'd like to also thank my children, Arthur and Lesley. It isn't always easy to have a writing mom (papers and notebooks everywhere!). It is, however, wonderfully easy to be their mother.

Thanks again for reading *Forgiven*. If you have a moment, please visit me on my website, www.shelleyshepardgray.com and tell me what you thought!

With God's Blessings to you,

*Shelley Shepard Gray*

# Questions for Discussion

1. The concept of truly forgiving resonates with several characters in this book. Have you ever had an instance where you, too, had a difficult time forgiving someone?

2. Winnie's search for love has been a rocky one. When she meets Sam again, she soon realizes he's the one for her. How did her past experiences lead her to be ready for a relationship with Sam?

3. Sam's journey took him away from the Amish community and back. Do you think he made the right choices?

4. More than ever, Caleb looks to his brothers for guidance. Eli and Samuel seem very different. Are they? What can Caleb learn from each brother?

5. The fire was a turning point in David's life. How do you think this episode will influence the rest of his life? How do you think it will influence his relationship with his father? With the Lord?

6. Was Jonathan right to not press charges against David?

7. What do you think the future holds for Anna? For her relationship with her parents?

SHELLEY SHEPARD GRAY is the beloved author of the Sisters of the Heart series, including *Hidden*, *Wanted*, and *Forgiven*. Before writing, she was a teacher in both Texas and Colorado. She now lives in southern Ohio where she writes full time.

**Center Point Publishing**
600 Brooks Road ● PO Box 1
Thorndike ME 04986-0001 USA

**(207) 568-3717**

**US & Canada:**
**1 800 929-9108**
www.centerpointlargeprint.com

Very good,